About the Author

Benny Jensen has worked as a clinical psychologist for over twelve years. Born and raised in Denmark, he has made his living in Greenland for the last five years, working as a therapist. An avid reader and gamer since early childhood, he also enjoys cultural experiences, travel, and nature; hence his current location in Greenland.

This Savage Cold Star

Benny Jensen

This Savage Cold Star

Vanguard Press

VANGUARD PAPERBACK

© Copyright 2024
Benny Jensen

The right of Benny Jensen to be identified as author of
this work has been asserted by him in accordance with the
Copyright, Designs and Patents Act 1988.

All Rights Reserved

No reproduction, copy or transmission of this publication
may be made without written permission.
No paragraph of this publication may be reproduced,
copied or transmitted save with the written permission of the
publisher, or in accordance with the provisions
of the Copyright Act 1956 (as amended).

Any person who commits any unauthorised act in relation to
this publication may be liable to criminal
prosecution and civil claims for damages.

A CIP catalogue record for this title is
available from the British Library.

ISBN 978 1 80016 913 5

This is a work of fiction. Names, characters, businesses, places, events and
incidents are either the product of the author's imagination or used in a
fictitious manner. Any resemblance to actual persons, living or dead, or
actual events is purely coincidental.

*Vanguard Press is an imprint of
Pegasus Elliot Mackenzie Publishers Ltd.*
www.pegasuspublishers.com

First Published in 2024

**Vanguard Press
Sheraton House Castle Park
Cambridge England**

Printed & Bound in Great Britain

I would like to dedicate this book to my mother and father, now long gone from this world. I hope you look upon me with pride, and love.

Prologue

In the Heart of Summer

The dreamscapes had been coming back for a while now, and Jannus Rubens knew it was time to suffer torment again. He woke up in the middle of the dark night, shaking with revulsion and sweating profusely, as he usually did after one of his ventures in the shaded purple and black dreamscape.

With rueful vexation he sat upright in bed, throwing the soaked night-blankets aside. The bedroom was dark and quiet with the exception of some video playing on his personal computer; it displayed a black screen with the sound of a brook or a stream, but with no images accompanying it. The recording was to provide comfort and relaxation, and Jannus experienced great difficulty resting or falling asleep without such methods.

While still sitting on the edge of his double bed (in which he always slept alone), Jannus reflected on this latest dreamscape. He had dreamt of a small stretch of land near some large body of water, maybe a fjord, covered in late summer snows. It had been night-time and dark, in his dream, though the scene was lit up by houselights, making the spectacle a weird blend of purple shadow and tawny gold. In his vision, he had looked up at the starless sky, and seen only interminable dark and shadow above him, finding no comfort in the night sky. And then the whispers had started to emanate from the houses, and the lights went out, one by one. And he knew, with the wisdom granted to him by the dreamworld, that he had to enter the red and white house at the end of the small village.

A pulsating ache in his right hand caught his attention; there was no blood, and no cuts, yet the back of his hand was partly black and purple, as if he had hit something hard. *Or the other way around,* Jannus thought with dismay, while the fading memory of the dreamscape echoed in his hand. He had been defending himself from some unknown assailant, stepping in and out of shadows, evading every countermove Jannus had to offer. After what had seemed like an endless battle, his opponent had retreated into the dark again, beyond sight, while Jannus had stood alone before the red and white house, door slightly ajar as if inviting him inside.

He had never had an effervescent personality by any means. 'A man of many opinions', 'quarrelsome to a fault' had been the usual descriptors by friends and family, and acquaintances. Admittedly, he had only a few of the former. Jannus knew that the latter was mostly beyond conjecture, considering him somewhat lacking in substance. Jannus knew differently, of course. He did admit to a certain degree of complacency, and he *did* have a certain tendency to casuistry, to his acquaintances' vast dismay.

After one of his nightly terrors, it was different though. It was as if he had suffered something traumatic, or some similar experience, that had changed him as a person. He knew, of course, due to his profession, that a personality change like that would be extremely rare, and not likely in his case. Jannus had been a therapist, yet only of middling quality in his own view; a nose-to-the-grindstone kind of worker, to be sure, yet always struggling and never excelling. He recalled a few of the positive recognitions he had achieved from co-workers and clients alike. He even believed most of them had been well-intentioned, if not exactly honest.

Jannus turned on the lamp on his nightstand, and sheltered his face with both hands until his eyes had adjusted to the sudden change. The much-too commodious bedroom was a mess, yet he did not pay it much attention. He opened the top drawer of the nightstand, and quickly found his medicine — his 'tranquilizers', as he called him, though the former therapist knew well enough that this was not their purpose, technically. A half-full glass of lukewarm water stood on the nightstand from the day before (or maybe the day previous to that), which he used to swallow today's medicine. Jannus hesitated a moment, and then gulped down tomorrow's tranquilizers as well. The dreamscape had been horrible, after all.

Leaving the bedroom, absently kicking aside any

clothes that might be in his way, he walked to the bathroom. The light flickered a few times when he turned it on, until it settled into a dull, yellow-orange glow. Jannus washed his face superficially, filling his left hand with water, and splashing his face a couple of times. He kept his right hand at his side. Using a towel that was still warm from lying folded on the top of the radiator, Jannus dried his face.

He caught his reflection in the bathroom mirror. It was not an easy task; the mirror had not been cleaned for at least a fortnight, and besides that it had been cracked a few times from past occasions when he had lost his temper. Jannus had never bothered to replace it. The result was that he found his own reflection looking back at him, broken in three, his emerald eyes full of sorrow caught in their own segment of the mirror. Other than that, he pretty much looked his age; a man almost in the middle of his forties, with burnt-umber, brown-coloured hair, turning to grey at the sides, and a dark stubble covering his neck and the lower half of his face. *Well, exactly my age,* he thought wryly. *My age if someone had taken really bad care of themselves.*

Almost recoiling from his own reflection, Jannus returned to the bedroom. After one of his dreams, he shifted from his complacent and casuistic self to a man humbler, and doubtful, and even fearful. As he waited for the medicine to gain momentum, and to return to the comfort of his false self, he reflected on one of his favourite lines of poetry: he wanted again to '*see the stars, and to course over better waters'.* Jannus could not remember the origin of the words, though they had remained at his side, even after his downfall. He knew not their exact importance, though he clung to them like a babe to his mother.

Jannus returned to sitting on his side of the bed, picking up some of the clothes that seemed least worn. He was not sure what usually prompted or elicited the dreamscapes. Jannus knew he had suffered from them almost all of his life, though he had never divined their starting point; though, admittedly, he had never truly tried. This time Jannus had an inkling of what had been the instigator. As he felt a certain calmness come over him, he stood up, and kicking aside three days' worth of unclean clothes, walked to the pinewood dresser. The middle drawer was half open, and one sock was hanging off the edge, threatening to join its partner on the carpeted floor. The object of his interest, however, lay on top of the drawer. An envelope he had procured from his mailbox, only two days ago. There had been a four-page letter inside. Jannus had read through only the first half-page before he realised what it was about, and he had left the envelope on the dresser, with two pages still sticking out.

Jannus looked around the dishevelled bedroom: used clothes spread all around, a double bed with the right half of it being neatly pressed linen, unlike its left counterpart. The sight made him both sad and angry.

He had read enough of the letter to suspect it might

be from an old client of his; the former therapist had identified the probable sender quickly, since the letter began by replicating one of the specific exercises they had worked on together. Jannus remembered the client and their sessions well. Too well, in fact. In Jannus' view, that time had been the beginning of his fall and his demise.

As he stood there, by his pinewood dresser, envelope in hand, wondering if he should read the rest of the letter inside, Jannus felt a strange sense of foreboding. It was as if his dreamscape had now entered his reality, whereas before, he never had any trouble distinguishing between the two. He looked at his right hand, still purple and black, and thought back to his ventures in the latest dreamscape. It was the heart of summer, and he was terribly afraid.

PART I

A LIFE OF AVOIDANCE

Chapter I

The Woman in King's Garden

A few days later, Jannus awoke with the dawn.

Looking outside his kitchen window, he saw an overcast sky, with just a small, cerulean blue opening at the eastern sky, the world's daystar in the middle, like a golden eye.

'Ah, let me gaze upon the star of spring, lay to rest at the lake of my heart', he murmured softly, while walking around restlessly in the kitchen, waiting for the morning coffee to be done. Jannus had his morning rituals, from which he rarely deviated. He considered them his last remnants of his daily structure. It looked to be a steel-grey day today, yet he had already convinced himself he would take a walk outside this morning. It had almost been a week since Jannus had walked out through his front door, just for leisure. He felt fresher today than the past few days.

Last night had been almost devoid of any sort of vision or dreamscape. Not that he could remember, anyway. And he could *always* remember. The only image that his memory had seemed to capture was the vision of a wooden bench outside the red and white house, almost completely covered by light snowfall. The image remained nonsensical to him.

He poured his coffee into his favourite mug (the one with the image of a woman in a crimson dress, holding a bucket of honey-yellow flowers). It had been his mother's. In accordance with heavy tradition, he added three spoonsful of sugar, and half an ounce of cream into his coffee. His former wife had complained several times that he put so much other stuff into his coffee, that maybe he did not actually like coffee at all? Maybe she had been right about that, like so many other things. *Ah these regrets,* he thought wistfully. *How easy to regret when you've fallen out of love.*

Jannus looked outside the kitchen window again. He saw his neighbours passing by — old Mr and Mrs Kearney, holding each other for support. They walked by very slowly. He felt his gut tighten a bit at the sight of them, though he did not follow through on the sensation. Jannus felt an inclination to retreat from the kitchen window; if they saw him, they might greet him, and maybe even want to engage him in conversation. The couple had always been inclined to conversation for as long as he had known them.

He knew old Mr Kearney had been quite a hunter in his younger years, and a fisherman, as well. The old man had seemingly lived quite a hard life, full of physical exertion, or so his wife had told Jannus, though she had never revealed her own former vocation. And Jannus had not asked.

The old couple walked around the corner, out of sight and out of mind. Jannus' thoughts returned to his own plan for the day, his once-a-week excursion into the savage world outside. He hoped the grey sky was not an ominous precursor to how the day would unfold. He put his waning hope into the small stretch of blue, and the daystar.

The kitchen was somewhat sparse, containing only the most basic commodities. He used to love to make quite elaborate dishes, though not to any great extent in the last couple of years. There was a table covered with a plastic tablecloth (showing red and green apples on a white backdrop), and a chair on either side of it. His dark brown coat lay across one of the chairs, and on the table, the mysterious envelope with the half-known content inside. Next to the envelope, Jannus had left this morning's newspaper, folded in half, today's headlines visible.

As he put on his coat, (and, almost absently, put the envelope in one of the front pockets), Jannus gazed at the newspaper headlines for today. He was not really much of a newspaper guy — never had been, to be honest — but he had succumbed to one of those subscription trials that promised a significant cut in the price for three months. They had also promised that the potential reader would be rewarded with fruitful discussion and debate, and insights into the issues of the day and the world. After two months' worth of reading the paper, Jannus surmised that what had been promised had proven mostly untrue. And furthermore, he had come to suspect that not buying the paper at all would have proven to be the cheapest cut of them all.

He walked outside into the savage world.

Today, the former therapist had decided to take a walk in the city park, which bore the illustrious name of King's Garden, though which king specifically, Jannus had forgotten. If it had been one of the warmongers, or one of the lovers of the sweet fruit of wine, he did not know. The garden was filled with all manner of flora and fauna, which Jannus *did* appreciate, on some level. It even held a small lake which you could walk around on a dirt path. A full circle would take him about fifteen minutes, at his current pace. He liked to take four turns, spending an hour in that manner, thus completing his weekly exercise. Sometimes, if the mood took him, he liked to take a short rest on one of the many benches the local council of Park and Recreation had so gently provided for the local citizenry. From there, he could watch the birds going about their daily life on the lake's surface (sometimes disappearing underneath), and watch while the gentle breeze embraced all the shades of green and orange and brown, and make everything sway in an accordance to an eternal dance.

And every season was different, too. Winter time was his favourite time in the garden, walking around the blue and black, frozen lake having an almost vitreous quality, and everything else being covered in white snow.

Jannus approached his favourite bench, the one in the shade by the great oak. In high summer it provided some much-needed shelter under its shadow. He did not need shelter this particular day, though, as the daystar showed itself only in glimpses behind the steel grey. Still, Jannus preferred this specific bench; a creature of habit he had thus become.

This part of the garden was almost empty this morning. Though the area was partially secluded from the rest of the city, and all the foliage protected somewhat from all the noise outside the garden, Jannus could still hear all the morning traffic. It was far enough away, thankfully, for him not to mind.

He *did* see an approaching figure though, coming from the far northern end of the garden. He had not seen anyone else, so whoever it was must have entered from the opposite entrance. *Or,* he reflected wryly, *maybe I just missed it, like so much else these days.* Jannus directed his gaze at a group of ducks who had walked onto land, and had started to walk across the dirt path in a long line, none of them walking side by side. There were even a few ducklings in the mix, walking dutifully behind the last adult. Jannus thought one or two of them might be looking his way, suspiciously, but he could not be sure. Despite himself, he was somewhat amused at the spectacle.

He felt a sudden shiver go through him, as a chill wind seemed to emerge from nothing, here in the shadow under the great tree. Jannus pulled his coat a bit tighter around himself. The envelope lay beside him on the bench. He had decided to read it today, but something made him hesitate. Though his current self-reflections were very much gravitating toward negativity, Jannus did not consider himself totally unconscionable, yet he did recognise that he had started to disconnect from the world around him; at one point or another he had started to disengage. And the first few lines of the first page of that letter had reminded him of that time when it all had seemed to descend.

At the sound of footsteps, Jannus looked up from the dreaded envelope beside him, and saw, for the first time, who had been making the journey around the lake this morning, just as he had. A woman in an indigo-blue coat was standing before him. She had short hair, mousy-grey, but she looked to be in her mid-thirties — somewhat younger than him. Her eyes were a startling grey, but not as the sky above: more like a pale silver, yet strangely warm, and comforting. The woman had stopped and looked at Jannus, with uncertainty. Belatedly, he realised she had asked him a question.

'Excuse me,' he began, somewhat embarrassed. 'Could you repeat that?'

The woman smiled at him (sadly, he thought), and repeated her question. 'Do you know the way to the railway station from here? I seem to have lost my way.'

Due to his long refrain from most human interaction and conversation, it took him a while to process the question, despite her repetition.

'Just walk out of the southern entrance, walk along Miller's Street for half a mile until you reach the old town square,' he managed to croak out.

He still felt a chill from the cold breeze, and he put a hand on the envelope beside him, as if afraid it would fly away with a sudden gust of wind. The woman in the indigo coat was looking at him, attentively. Jannus looked back at her, now uncertain of himself.

'And I think,' he said, with some hesitation, 'that you should go right across the square, past the bank and the goldsmith on your left, and leave by *that* street. I don't know the name of that street, though,' he finished, now partly irritated, both at himself *and* the woman with her inane questioning.

She seemed to look at him appreciatively, though, and she smiled at him in a manner he managed to interpret as kind and thankful.

'Thank you,' she said, and nodded in a southerly direction. 'I think I can find my way now,' she continued, while already taking steps in the direction she wanted. 'Besides,' she said over her shoulder, with her pale silver eyes, 'I'll just ask around at the town square if I get confused.'

With sure steps she walked out of King's Garden, leaving Jannus to his solitude, thinking of all the things he wanted to have said.

He sat in quiet reflection a few minutes after the woman had left. Partly, Jannus felt relief for the unknown woman's absence. Yet he also felt a certain kind of emptiness or absence as she left the Garden, and left him. Irritated at himself, Jannus picked up the envelope with some force, and pulled out the pages within.

What had made the first few lines immediately recognisable was that it was his own handwriting. He had asked his former client to do an exercise, where he had to write out a farewell letter to his sister — or had it been his mother? Whatever the case might have been, the client had been too emotionally distraught to do so. They had agreed that Jannus, as the therapist, would write out the words that the client spoke, and then the latter would read it out loud, to make it more manifest.

I miss you so much, the letter began. *Every day without you hurts. I was supposed to protect you, but I could not. I was supposed to help you. But didn't. I don't know what do to now, without you.*

Jannus looked up at the sound of some rustling behind him. It was only the family of ducks on their return from wherever, back to the waters. He studied the envelope. There had not been an address of any sort on the envelope; not even a name. Which meant that someone probably had put the envelope in his mailbox, personally. He shivered. A personal note? A *threat?* Jannus was unsure of the right procedure in a case such as this.

Back to the content of the letter, he thought he now knew who the lost person was. It must have been his client's sister. It still remained elusive in which manner she had died. An accident? Natural causes, or suicide? After more than ten years as a therapist, his memory of most of his clients had become diluted. The details he might think belonged to one client would, in reality, be attributed to someone else entirely. The former therapist kept reading.

Remember when we used to go ice skating on the fjord? In the winter, when the waters were frozen and solid? You were so nervous, but I helped you then, remember? I helped you then. One time, you fell on the ice, with me standing on land. When I saw, I ran as fast as I could, nervous that you would fall through. But the ice had remained solid. We went back to the house for warm cocoa, and wrapped blankets around us.

Jannus had asked his client to talk about one of his favourite moments with his sister; something that he would keep with him, close to his heart, after her unfortunate passing. As the last miniscule duckling had entered the waters of the lake, Jannus began to remember his client more clearly. His client had been very clever, with quite an intriguing personality, and distinguished in his own way. Yet there had been a certain darkness to him that had been unexplainable to him. As far as Jannus remembered, the client had broken off their sessions after this exercise, and had never returned to the therapy room. The letter had meant to bring his client conclusion and resolution of a sort, but he was uncertain if it had ever done so.

I will remember your smile, and your laughter, and your trust in me. Even though I failed that trust in the end, I hope you know I always loved you. And I hope you'll forgive me before my time comes. I'll strive to be as good as I can be, maybe even a hero, like you thought me to be. Your 'gentleman of leisure', as you so cleverly named me. Lux upon lux, lux in tenebris, my dear. My love is eternal.

And there the letter ended. Almost. At the bottom on the fourth and last page, someone had added something in slightly different writing with a different colour pen. It looked sloppy, yet somehow aggressive. It looked to be an address of some sort, not immediately familiar to Jannus. If he had seen the address before, it was buried deep in his memory. Despite the day warming up — the sun had finally seemed to break through the heavy clouds — he felt another shiver. Was the envelope put in the mailbox by his old client? Was it his address? Jannus knew he should feel afraid, yet he felt strangely detached. His former wife had always told him that he was paradoxically calm in his fatalism.

Still uncertain how to proceed, he put the envelope back in his coat pocket, and walked to the edge of the lake. You were not meant to feed the wildlife in the garden. There were instructions not to do so placed in several locations around the park,. Apparently, the park was self-sufficient, so guests (mostly, the local populace) were not required to bring their own supplements. Most people Jannus had seen actually adhered to that, though once in a while he succumbed to the temptation himself, bringing some stale bread along.

At the lake's edge he looked down on his reflection in the water. The day had brightened enough so that Jannus could see almost a mirror image of himself, with the daystar over his shoulder, still determined to break through. He looked at a sad and tired, unshaven face, and unkempt hair. Jannus had not bothered with either for some time now. As he straightened up, and his mirror image was lost to sight, he decided to walk back home again, rather than take a couple of circuits around the lake. He had spent whatever energy had been at his disposal this day. He had hoped for more.

And in a dark corner, buried deep, the gentleman of leisure grinned his ugly smile, reflecting the ugly soul within. He had felt himself stirring these last couple of days. He had felt something coming: something light, and something dark. He had finally found a path; a way forward, something to aspire to do. He had to go back to that place, that place of no return. That place in the ice and snow, where you could fall through, where you might lose someone if you were not careful. The gentleman of leisure had learned just that: he had learned just what to do, to get what he wanted, what he needed. Whatever it took for him to become a hero. He had only to wait for someone to come along.

Chapter II

Last Embers

A couple of days later, Jannus found himself preoccupied with trying to clean up some of the mess in the house. He got rid of all the clothes on the bedroom floor, which, to his great chagrin, revealed all the wine and beer-stain spots on the carpet underneath. Gone were the bottles on the coffee table in the living room, and there was no evidence left of the dishes with the three days' worth of dried and hardened food stains. After all this work, his energy for the day was spent. And it was not even noon.

Lying flat on the black leather couch, feeling somewhat proud of his meagre accomplishment, Jannus stared up at the ceiling. He knew it was not going to be the last time he was going to clean up the chaos he had created. His lessons in life had always been hard-won. As a kid — and even as a young man — he had often got into fights, including physical altercations. A few times he had limited himself to the verbal variation; a variation on a theme, really.

His parents had been called to quite a few meetings at the school.

'Your son has quite a temper,' they would say, while his parents both nodded, his mother expressing regret, and even his father had looked contrite — falsely, most likely. Jannus had known even then, that it did not fit with how his father would act in any other setting, and he had never quite understood his father's behaviour in that particular venue.

He remembered one of these occasions in particular, if only for the presence of his most loathed teacher. Looking back, most of his teachers had been decent; a few of them even great. But one of them, Mr Wilkinson, had been the worst of them. He had been one of those teachers whose only remaining tool was venomous irony. And so, while the good Mr Wilkinson had expounded upon all of the virtues lacking in little Jannus, in a manner most injudicious (in little Jannus' view), his parents had just kept nodding, as non-committal as ever.

'Why, we'll make sure to talk with Jannus when we get home, Principal,' they had said. The principal in question had nodded in satisfaction, and all was well and good.

Jannus had never liked it at home, or at school. His only haven had been when he would visit a friend, or he was out in the wilds, amidst nature, away from people. *Ironically, I became a therapist then,* he thought, while still staring at the ceiling. He spent quite a few hours every day looking at that living room ceiling. Or so it seemed to Jannus. Maybe because it did not require too much of him: no expectations or failed aspirations came to life by just looking at your living room ceiling. This specific activity also gave him plenty of time to think.

'Remember, Jan,' his grandmother had once said to him, 'time spent thinking is time well spent!' While he did not doubt her words had been well-intentioned, he was not sure if he agreed. He always thought of her with great affection, though. She had been of his few true supporters in his early life, in his opinion; one of the few lights in the dark amidst all the terrible.

'Well there, little Jan, what have you been up to?' she would always ask him when he showed up at her door, with a school bag on his back containing his text books, and a bag in his hand full of a few days' worth of clothes. She had looked upon him with great compassion, and a little worry at the corner of her eyes.

'I just wanted to visit, Grandma,' he chose to answer. Much later, as a therapist, he would realise how loyal children would be to their parents, even if it were not reciprocated. At the end of his career, just a few years ago now, Jannus had mostly lost his sense of empathy. But when he had been faced by the prospect of someone betraying the trust of a child, he would still get riled.

'Being committed emotionally does not mean you should be overwhelmed by the therapeutic clients,' he had once learned. *'But it should mean that you are invested in the person in front of you, and whatever issue you are presented with.'* Well, Jannus had tried to,

at least, for as long as he could.

The sound of a dog barking outside broke Jannus from his reverie. He had left the door to his garden open to get in some fresh hair, and to cleanse the house of some of that beer and wine and leftover food smell. He stood up from the couch, stretched to the tip of his toes, and walked to the open door, the curtains fluttering a bit from the slight breeze travelling through. 'Garden' was a bit of a misnomer: he used to have an expansive knowledge of and interest in flora, yet now the garden was really just a patch of grass, about six squares of it. He had thought about using the garden space for something, but had never gotten around to it. An eight-foot-high hedge surrounded the small garden, providing some privacy from the outside, if you wanted to enjoy some time without passing people looking in. There was no respite from the sound of barking, though. And there were a lot of dog owners in this neighbourhood, Jannus and his former wife had noticed, when they moved in all those years ago.

'I'm not sure I like it here, Jan,' she had said to him once. When she had called him 'Jan', it felt very different to when his grandmother had once called him that. It warned of a shift of mood, a change in pace, and of a possible conflict coming up.

'What don't you like about it, dear?' he had said back then, looking up from his theory books. Maybe he had put the wrong emphasis on 'dear', since she had walked into his workroom, wearing a serious expression on her face. He had never liked that look: it reminded him of someone he once knew.

While he had sat at his desk, with computer screen and a pile of books in front of him, she had listed all the things she had not liked. With one hand on her hip, and one foot tapping in synchronicity, she had given her tirade. Jannus still remembered it, word for word. *This whole neighbourhood, the neighbours* (Mrs Kearney, in particular, he knew), *the noise, and the lack of light, too much space, and there's too far a distance to anything, Jan!'* He had been wise enough not to mention that it had been her idea to move here, especially since she had ended her outburst with tears in her eyes.

'There's too many shadows here, Jan,' she muttered. 'Too many shadows.'

And since Jan knew all about shadows, he had agreed with her. That had been one of their last discussions; the last embers of their life together.

They had had their share of fights, as husband and wife, Jan reflected, standing at the garden door. The dog barking had subsided, and he was left in silence with only the slight breeze for comfort. He had enough insight to know that he had himself partly to blame for those fights. Sometimes Jannus just could not contain his temper, and he would say something stupid, or unwarranted. Especially when she had said something which had spoken to some truth hidden deep inside.

Some days he rejoiced in his solitude; other days he lamented her absence.

Jannus walked away from his little garden and his memories, through the living room, and opened the door to his old study. It consisted of no more than a few square feet, even smaller than the garden, but with just enough room for a desk — solid, practical and simple — and a bookshelf leaning against the opposite wall. The shelf was brimming over with books, naturally, but the desk was empty, except for his old laptop. In the old days, the desk would have been covered with books of theory and mind. After a normal workday, he would usually come in here, and keep himself and his mind occupied. As a general rule, he would wake up once per week in the middle of the night, with one cheek planted on an open book, his reading glasses consequently at an odd angle. Most other days he would stop himself (or his former wife would) reading at around ten or eleven in the evening, and then he would go to sleep in a proper bed. A lot of his life had been books once. Now all of them had found their way onto the shelf, forever closed under a thick layer of dust. Jannus went to his laptop on the desk, and opened it, and pressed the start button. Nothing happened. After a moment of confusion, he discovered that the power was not connected. *Then the battery must be empty too,* he thought with some amusement.

It was of little consequence; there was nothing on that laptop that would be of interest, anyway. One of the prime things Jannus had learned, during his vocation, was that you should not, if possible, ever take your work home with you. Both in a literal sense, naturally, but also in a more cognitive and emotional way. While helping others, you should also take care to look after yourself. Jannus knew that quite a few of his former peers sometimes forgot that sort of self-care; especially when times were stressful, and you just forgot about yourself. When he was not wallowing in too much self-sympathy, the former therapist was well aware that he also had forgotten part of himself along the way. Not that he had meant to do so, of course. You never do.

Starting yesterday, Jannus had taken only the medication prescribed to him in terms of the daily dosage. He did not feel any immediate change; not that he had noticed, anyway. Yet it *did* seem that his thoughts were not as muddled as they had been for what had felt like a very long time. The house looked different to him, somehow. It looked dark and full of shadows, almost as though no light was allowed to come in from the outside. He had not even discerned that most of the light *in* the house had been turned off, as well. He must have lived in darkness for many days. When this realisation had dawned on him, Jannus had turned on all the lights, almost as if he had compensated for those many days without it. It still seemed like an anomaly with all that brightness around him; part of him felt exposed, and he wanted to hide away in the shadows again, as if they were a comfortable blanket for him to wear.

But looking in the mirror this very morning, he also

noticed a change. The image was clearer than the one he had seen on the lake's surface a few days ago, despite the broken glass. He saw, again, the tired face, and all the unwanted lines that spoke of exhaustion and regret; he saw eyes of emerald green looking back at him with broken hope. Jannus had jerked away from the mirror at this point, emotionally overwhelmed by something inside that threatened. *Not now, not now,* he had gasped, and pleaded, and had tried to complete his morning ritual.

Jannus closed the door to his old study room. He was not yet ready to dive back into that world of theory and mind. One day at a time, as he had often advised his clients. He walked into his bedroom. He had made his bed this morning, also for the first time in quite a while. His gaze went to the letter, still in its place, and untouched since the day in the park. He was still unsure how to proceed. Should he call the authorities? There was not really an implicit threat in the wording of the letter.

He picked up the envelope, now in hand unbandaged. Jannus did not have an extensive knowledge of what different types of envelopes there were, only that they came in different sizes for different purposes. But now, having gone through the initial confusion, he had noticed certain peculiarities. For one, the envelope seemed somewhat deeper than normal, and it had a large, pointed flap, compared to what an ordinary envelope should have. That was his impression, anyway.

The *why* of it eluded him, though. The only content in the envelope was the four-page letter. Maybe the sender did not have any other kind of envelope... Jannus had even thought of looking up the address, just out of curiosity. It would be the easiest thing in the world, and perhaps, looking at a map in front of him would provide some sort of answer. He remained reluctant to do so, however. Something made him hesitate, and stay his hand.

And the dreamscapes had been returning more extensively, as well. The dreamscape a week ago had been almost a singular occurrence; it was as if the visions had left him. For years he had been without them, partly to his relief, since they disturbed him greatly. Yet Jannus also felt a certain hollowness without them, like something had been missing, which he did not comprehend. He had hardly ever felt the dreamscapes had helped him in any shape or form. As a child he would never tell his parents about them, and he would have kept his silence if any one of them would have deigned to ask him, in the morning, why he looked so pale, or why his sheets were soaked in sweat. They never had.

One time, when visiting his grandmother, he had talked about them in a veiled manner. He did not tell her about the dreams, specifically, but he had dared to ask her if she thought dreams meant anything at all. She had looked up from her knitting (another pair of homemade socks, if Jannus had it right), sitting in her grand boysenberry-coloured armchair, and looked at him kindly, though a bit suspiciously. Maybe she had sensed there was something wrong, and to her credit, there usually was.

'Why, I do not know, Jan. I do not dream so much any more, my dear,' she had said. His grandmother had looked out her window then, at a world she no longer could keep up with. Even little Jan was cognisant of her reluctance in giving him an answer. She had looked back at him with just a hint of fright in her eyes. Jan thought her hands had even trembled a bit, the knitting needles clacking together softly. 'As a little girl I had plenty of dreams, my dear,' she had said. 'Most of them were not true, though a few…' And then she had trailed off.

Back then, Jannus had not asked her any more, since he did not want to make her sad or angry. If she became sad or angry, then maybe he would have to leave and go back home again. And little Jan would have gone to great lengths not to go home again for as long as he could. Now, though, Jannus wished he had asked her what she had meant. He had spent most of his adult life trying to run away from the dreamscapes, trying to numb himself even, to make them disappear. Once in a while they would pop up again, rearing their ugly head, assuring him that they would always be there.

Jannus looked around his clean-for-the-first-time-in-a-while bedroom, and grimaced. He could clean up his room and his house well enough, but dealing with all the chaos inside was a different matter. Jannus sat down on the edge of the bed, letter still in hand, and laughed softly. *The irony of a therapist who cannot deal with his own mental issues,* he thought, not for the first time. Though he supposed it was not a unique thing; he himself had had several of his peers in for counselling. Some schools of thought recommended that you would at least try to be a client yourself, just to get the experience and the perspective. So, to some extent, it *did* make sense, that *of course* you could have issues yourself, as a therapist. You just had to deal with them as anyone else did, and be aware if those issues provided any sort of obstacle to give the correct sort of counsel to the individual client.

So far, so good. Yet these dreamscapes had haunted him for decades now, without Jannus even having tried to deal with them, except for pushing them away in less constructive ways. During his former career, he had also had quite a few clients who had liked to discuss their dreams in different ways. Some just liked to talk about them in a general manner as an experience of sorts. Other people saw them as symbolic, or meaningful on a deeper level. For Jannus, in the role of a therapist, he had mostly seen their dreams as normal; that is, just a way for the brain to clean up the memory banks. He was more interested in what the clients *thought* of their dreams. What *they* thought they meant, or signified.

That was usually the more interesting aspect in his view. It often spoke of some underlying issue, mentally or emotionally; some other conflict that the client had a difficult time expressing in their daily lives, but still had an effect. He never said to a client that their dreams did not mean anything in themselves, or that he did not perceive them to embody any kind of prophetic quality. That could possibly ruin their working relationship, their therapeutic alliance. But he would direct their attention toward what *he* thought was the real issue at hand. So, there was some degree of subterfuge going on, he had to admit.

Jannus was also aware of his relation to his own dreams. And that most of the time, he also had what he would classify as 'normal' dreams; or within the realm of normalcy, at least. But the dreamscapes were different somehow, though it remained difficult for Jannus to ascertain why. Maybe it was because they seemed more real or tangible. *Physical,* almost. Like he was actually at the place in the dream, though he knew that was impossible, of course. The main division between normal dreams and his dreamscape was the fact that he felt an imminent sense of *danger* in the dreamscape, both when sleeping, but also a few days after. It felt like something was approaching, something unwanted, and dangerous; *lethal* to himself and his soul. *No wonder he had tried to keep them away, then.*

As Jannus looked around his cleaned-up bedroom again, he felt a sudden urge to mess it all up once more, like he always used to. Part of him wanted to go back to that place of shadow and no light, and leave it all be. A clean house meant no distractions in a strange way; it meant that more room was left for himself. And that had always been the most dangerous thing of all for Jannus.

And in his dark solitude, the gentleman of leisure heard the cries of exultation. Part of him wanted to escape that savage place, yet he remained lost in the fog. He had suffered, been the victim of eternal maledictions, Once, he had been an individual of great vivacity and verdure. He had been a climber of delectable mountains. Yet, here he was in his solitude, in the dark, beaten and scarred, and cold from the touch of treachery. And still he watched, and waited.

Chapter III

Mourning on a Tuesday

Jannus awoke early the next morning to the gentle patter of summer rain on his window, and an insistent knocking on his front door. He tumbled out of bed, tripped over his night blanket, and hit his head on the wall. He stood there, dazed from just waking up, and the pain in his skull. Jannus would have kept standing there, cradling his poor head, if not for another knock at the door.

Who can it be at this hour? he wondered, walking drunkenly out of the bedroom. Luckily, his sleep had been mostly dreamless. Only a few images had survived to his waking memory. *A bird wing, cracked and folded. A reindeer out in front of a house, red and white. And his grandmother, looking out of her window, which was all she did at the end of her life, warming her hands by the radiator, looking over her shoulder at the last remaining light.*

Jannus finally reached his door, and opened it only a few inches wide. This neighbourhood was safe enough, yet it never hurt to be too careful. But when he looked out, it was only old Mrs Kearney, from next door, one fist in the air ready to knock one more time.

'Mrs Kearney? What are you doing here?' Jannus thought she looked sad and frightened. And it looked like she was crying, though that could have been the rain.

Mrs Kearney did not answer right away, as she looked him up and down. Belatedly, he realised he was still wearing his underwear, and a T-shirt. For the latter, he was somewhat grateful.

'Mr Rubens,' the old lady began.

'Jannus,' he said.

She tried to finish her sentence, but could not. She just stood there in the rain, looking at Jannus. Slightly irritated (not at the old woman, but at his own aching head, and his own clumsiness), he opened the door a little wider.

'Is there something wrong, Mrs Kearney? Something wrong with your husband?'

The old woman's lips quivered, and she finally broke into tears. For the first time, Jannus noticed the red around her eyes, and that she was only dressed in a skinny nightgown, despite the morning rain. Suddenly, Mrs Kearney took a few steps forward, and embraced him, her face against his chest. On any other day, Jannus would most likely have held the old woman out at arm's length, being uncomfortable with such displays of compassion. But maybe it was the thoughts and dreams of his own grandmother that softened his stance and his heart to Mrs Kearney. Her grey, curly hair, darkened somewhat from the rain, tickled his chin, but he ignored it, and put two arms around her, and let her cry. Still with his arms around her, he walked with her inside the house, and closed the door behind them.

About half an hour later, they sat together in his kitchen. Jannus had made them both a mug of coffee. He had offered her cream and sugar to go with it, only to realise he had supplies of neither. By chance, she had declined both, to his relief. While he was busy brewing, she had told him in stops and starts what had happened to her husband.

Apparently, he had sequestered (Jannus had frowned at Mrs Kearney's choice of words, but had refrained from any comment, unwanted and unnecessary as it would have been) himself in their bedroom, and locked the door.

'I did not even know we had a key, Mr Rubens,' she said, looking at him in desperate need for answers. Jannus had seen that look many times in a more professional setting. He had gently asked her to call him Jannus a couple of times, but for now, she seemed to prefer formalities. Jannus had seen that, too: when things went to hell, people reacted in all manner of ways. Some people, like Mrs Kearney, apparently, fell back to their old ways and standards, both in action and expression.

'I did not think anything was afoot at first, Mr Rubens,' she had elaborated, cradling the coffee mug in both hands, his night blanket over her frail shoulders. 'I did not even know the door was locked until I wanted to go to bed myself, you see?' Jannus had simply nodded his understanding, knowing she only required his immediate presence. 'But then I knocked and knocked, and nothing happened,' she had said, her eyes brimming with tears again, though this time without spilling a drop. 'After half an hour of knocking, I called our daughter, Eleanora. She told me to call the authorities.' The old lady had looked at Jannus almost apologetically at this point. 'She lives far away you see, on the other side of the coast, so she cannot always help as much as she wants, you see?'

Maybe Mrs Kearney thought he had needed some convincing, since she had added, 'Otherwise, I'm sure she would have moved with great alacrity to help me, don't you think, Mr Rubens?' Her look of desperation and need for answers was back again, in full force.

'I'm sure she would, Mrs Kearney. I'm sure she would.' Jannus had no idea what Eleanora would or would not do, but the old woman seemed satisfied with his answer.

'Yes, she was always a sweet girl, Mr Rubens, though surreptitious to a fault at times!' Mrs Kearney had finally let go of the coffee mug and had put it on the kitchen table. At this point the old woman had seemed to settle down just a bit. She had gone on to talk about how the police had come to her house ('It took ages, Mr Rubens. Ages, I tell you'), and broken down the bedroom door ('It only took them a few pushes to break down that old thing'). Inside, they had found old Mr Kearney, lying in bed, sleeping, never to awake. After this reveal, Mrs Kearney had not spoken for a while.

Now the morning rains had finally stopped outside, raindrops gently rolling down the kitchen window. On the sill stood an ancient elephant figurine, caparisoned in a red and black crochet. His grandmother had been something of a collector of figurines, and her favourite animal had been the elephant. When she passed away, a select few of them had been dispersed among family members, but most of them had gone the way of charity.

'Will you be all right now, Mrs Kearney?' Jannus asked softly. The old woman did not answer right away. Patiently, he gave her the needed time: the former therapist knew that she would be a jumble of emotions right now, most likely. Her curly hair had dried up somewhat and had now attained a softer grey nuance. She had taken the borrowed blanket from her shoulders and it was lying in her lap, with her hands underneath, still seeking warmth and comfort.

'Yes, I'll be fine, Mr Rubens. I think.' She looked outside. 'Our daughter should be here tomorrow, if she makes her flight. I just don't know…' She trailed off again, and yet again Mr Rubens did not pressure her with too many questions or unneeded information.

'Will you be all right until tomorrow again?' he asked her. 'Until your daughter shows up?'

She nodded absently.

From what Jannus understood, the old man had just put himself to bed, and never woken up. Had he known he would die? Jannus did not reflect too much on his own mortality, but he would prefer that when the time came, he would pass away in his sleep, unaware of what was about to happen to him. But how had the old man known, if he knew at all? And if not, why would he lock the bedroom door, with only him and his wife living in the house? Jannus was somewhat surprised by himself; despite his own current travails, he felt quite invested in helping the old woman in *her* current situation. At least in so far as making sure she was safe until tomorrow — until her daughter would hopefully arrive.

Maybe it was not so strange: quite often, people would focus on other people's issues or troubles, all the while they were mired in their own. The former was sometimes easier. Jannus had seen this a lot in his former career; he had held sessions with people with all manner of psychological and social issues; people with depression or some form of anxiety, or even personality disorders or chronic conditions. People were different, whatever category of those you could put them in, yet what had often struck him was their ability to have sufficient mental resources to have empathy or sympathy for others, despite suffering themselves. Part of this was self-serving, naturally. To focus on something rather than your own suffering could be seen as seeking relief, if only for a short while.

As if the old woman sitting in his kitchen had read

his mind, she suddenly asked, 'And how are *you* doing, Mr Rubens?'

Jannus looked at her, and her expression seemed genuine, and caring. Again, she reminded him a bit of his own grandmother, lost to the world for many years now. Still, he was not ready for her to shift the attention back to him so rapidly. Jannus was not accustomed to someone actually showing him this sort of sympathetic attention, having it directed toward him. It had always been an uncomfortable sensation, and usually, preferably, he would rather have gone without.

'We haven't seen you for a good while, Mr Rubens. Me and my husband, I mean.' Mrs Kearney took another sip from her mug, the coffee most likely lukewarm by now. She did not seem to mind, or maybe she did not sense it at all.

'I'm all right, Mrs Kearney,' he said, dishonestly, partly because he did not know what to say; partly because he did want to bother her. He had always been this way — not wanting to bother other people.

'Just a bit under the weather, lately,' Jannus continued, which he supposed was true in some sense. He added a smile, just for effect. The old woman gave him a shrewd look, as if she knew something was not quite right. She put her coffee mug back on the table, but kept a hand on the grip.

'Well, all right then,' she said, still with a look of slight disbelief. Jannus had come to suspect that the old woman was quite discerning, despite her current condition. Jannus looked out of the window again, so he could escape that penetrating gaze. The morning sky was suffused with a soft red and yellow glow. 'Not too long ago, my husband remarked on just how long it had been since we've seen you about, Mr Rubens. He was worried about you, you know?'

This came as a surprise to Jannus, and he looked back to the old woman. 'He did?'

Mrs Kearney nodded. 'Oh yes, oh yes. Most definitely! Why, it was just the other day that he made the notion "Oh that Mr Rubens, what a stellar individual, wouldn't you say, my dear? A stellar individual."'

'Why, that was very kind of him,' Jannus almost stuttered, guiltily, thinking of how he had tried to avoid the old couple just the other morning. He had not wanted them to disturb his walk, if he recalled correctly. 'I'm sorry I did not get to know him more than I did, Mrs Kearney,' he managed.

The old woman looked at him appreciatively, and smiled. Jannus thought she looked like she was gathering courage to say something that he might *not* appreciate.

'I'm sure he would have loved that,' she said, both hands again hidden under the borrowed blanket. Once again, her look became sympathetic. "It's just that — well, we thought we had not seen you for so long because of what happened between you and your wife, Mr Rubens. We remember her fondly, you see.' Mrs

Kearney seemed a bit embarrassed that she had perhaps unveiled too much.

I remember her, too, he thought. *I remember the first time I saw her, silver dress almost diaphanous as she swirled and twirled, her long dark wavy hair tumbling about her shoulders. I remember her, too.*

'Oh, I'm sorry, Mr Rubens! I did not mean to make you upset!' The old woman left her chair and came over to stand next to him by the kitchen counter. 'Oh, here I am, making a nuisance of myself!' Mrs Kearney seemed to be scolding herself. 'And here you are, trying to help me!' The old woman took his face in both hands, one on each side, and held his eyes. 'I thank you, Mr Rubens, for you opening your door and your home to me today.' Maybe she could feel him struggling to look away, since she tightened her hold with surprising strength. 'I *know* you have your own things to take care of, my dear. And I truly hope you get them sorted out.'

Mrs Kearney took a few steps back, and smiled at him, a single tear running down her cheek. 'My husband was right, you know; you *are* a stellar individual.' Lost for words, Jannus just nodded and looked down at his own two feet, bare on the kitchen floor. He could still hear her last words as she prepared to leave him, and go back to her own house. 'I just hope you can see that, too, one day.'

A few hours after the old woman had left the house to go back to her own place to wait for her daughter,

Jannus felt a strange emptiness, a certain hollowness, inside. Or rather, he felt something inside from a place he *thought* would be empty, what he had considered as hollow. Ever quick to identify any kind of emotional indicator, as per his vocation, Jannus thought he knew what this particular sensation was about. For a relatively long time, he had remained isolated from other people, mostly by his own volition. As he sat on a chair in his minimalistic back garden, enjoying the smell of grass after the rainfall, Jannus was contemplating his different life choices over the last couple of years.

'It seems like the old woman triggered something,' he muttered, looking around his mostly empty garden. *A bit like my life*, he mused, on this day of mourning. For the last two hours, he had wondered why the death of old Mr Kearney had affected him as much as it had; maybe it was more the reaction of his widow, which was quite relatable. But he had not really interacted with them all that much. Not since the time when he could call himself a husband, and his whole world had seemed broader; at least in terms of how many people he would get to meet. Most of that had vanished when the divorce had hit.

'No, that's not true,' Jannus almost whispered, in the empty garden. 'Not entirely.'

He chuckled, despite himself. He had developed a habit of talking to himself, since living alone. *A prerogative of the elderly and the lonely,* he thought, ruefully. The only things of import in the garden were the chair he was currently occupying, a small, deep-green garden table next to it, and a big, red utility box that had stood silently against the house wall, untouched for at least two years. Supposedly, the thing was filled with all manner of tools for possible use in this very garden. Jannus had never had any sort of inclination toward this sort of work. It was not that he thought it beneath him, or that he lacked the affinity for it. He just did not have the interest.

'Or so I've always told myself,' Jannus said, as he lifted his mug of coffee from the garden table and took a sip. He reflected that coffee had remained his sole source of stimulant, if you didn't count the prescribed medication, which was technically not a stimulant, as such. And they certainly did not feel that way for Jannus. They worked much more as inhibitors do, especially if devoured in too large a dose. He supposed this was a positive development of sorts, a return to life in a way; at least in the way that life was now. Not optimal in any way, but decent enough. Adequate. He had brought the envelope out here in the garden with him. It was currently residing on the garden table next to his coffee. Jannus had read it two or three more times, since he had decided to come out here after the morning rains had subsided completely. He had dried off the chair with a cloth, made another brew, grabbed the envelope almost as an afterthought, and had spent a couple of hours out here, just relaxing, and reflecting.

One of the notions Jannus had come upon in his

reflections was how little of that he had done these recent years. In fact, it had become clearer to him how much effort he had put into *avoiding* exactly that. Strange, considering how he had always considered his ability to reflect and see the same incident from every sort of angle as a great strength. Not only personally, but also in his work-life. It had proved most effective in working with all sorts of people with all sorts of backgrounds and life stories. Almost no matter where people came from, he had the ability to empathise. And most importantly, he used to know how to make other people *know* that they were understood, and that someone, in a genuine way, wanted to help them. What he still did not possess the answer to, though, was how or why he had lost those abilities; whether he was the source of their absence himself, or if someone had taken them away from him.

Later, that evening, Jannus fell asleep hoping he would get a good night's sleep, free from any sort of dreamscapes or premonitions. But that night, they returned in truth.

The gentleman of leisure was angry. Angry at himself and angry at the world. Mostly the latter. He was mad at the one who had so easily disposed of his heart; he reviled those who had made a mockery of his intellect. Still kept in the dark in his hall of mirrors, the gentleman was mad at all those people along his way, who had never followed his precepts, who had never given him their time of day. He remembered all their smiling faces, remember how they had laughed and pointed. Yet, strangely, for all of his second sight, he never saw those who had cried when he fell.

Chapter IV

Along the Darkened Shore

In his dreamscape, Jannus was standing near a coastline. There were no sounds of waves crashing; the waters were completely still and silent. Everything was suffused in a dark, purple shadow, except a small point in the sky, coloured white and blue. Just half a mile ahead of him was the small village; the one he had seen before. Jannus looked down at himself; he was dressed simply, in blue jeans, and a white shirt. On his feet a pair of solid boots, as if he had prepared for a hard excursion on difficult terrain.

He was curious as to what lay before him; were there people in the village? If so, were they waiting for him? Could he talk to them? It had been quite a few years since he had been motivated to learn more about his dreams, so he had difficulty remembering what he could and could not do, while in the dreamscape. He was still nervous, still hesitant, about proceeding. But to his own surprise, Jannus found himself just a bit curious as well. As a child he had wanted to be something of an adventurer; to go on an epic quest of some sort. He had absolutely loved books and games as a child, mostly as another much-needed refuge for his assailed mind. Child-Jannus had wanted to travel into the world of books, somewhere far away from the reality surrounding him. "You will meet enemies three," someone mysterious and mythical would direct him, and on he would go. Sadly, life had proven not to be the sort of quest he had wished for.

Jannus started walking toward the village, when he noticed a huge iceberg passing by in the waters to his left. An iceberg that had not been there just a few seconds before, he was sure of it. The iceberg looked to be slowly travelling down the silent waters, somehow. A couple of seagulls flew by, looking miniscule against the icy backdrop. To his right, he saw what looked to be an endless (as far as he could see, anyway) dry plain, with no hint of civilisation, no buildings or road or anything.

There seemed to be nothing interesting for him in that direction. *Well, almost nothing,* he thought, as something on the dry plains caught his attention. Three little figures, no higher than small children, were walking in a straight line. They were too far away for him to make out their faces, yet he could tell they were dressed in colourful clothing, like three court jesters. Their movements looked almost like they were dancing, or at least moving to some rhythm or harmony beyond his own hearing. At first, Jannus thought the group was moving in his direction, but then they turned around and moved away in a direction away from him. In silence he watched the procession for a while, until he discovered that they seemed to be walking a triangle-shaped path, walking from corner to corner, again and again. Just as Jannus was about to call out to them, they disappeared from his sight.

Perplexed, Jannus shook his head, and turned his attention back to the village by the shore. It looked be relatively isolated, and deserted. As Jannus was getting closer and closer, he could feel tension rising, even though he only walked at a steady pace. He was curious, yes, but still careful. Though previous events from his dreamscapes were buried deep in his mind and his heart, he was dimly aware of something potentially dangerous. And there was a certain unease in the air. It was *too* silent, as if the world here itself were afraid to make a sound. From his current vantage point, the village consisted of about fourteen or fifteen houses, most of them situated alongside a middle road with five houses on either side, and two bigger buildings just beyond that. Jannus thought one of them might serve as a town hall; the other one looked to be more open-spaced and lacking walls, like a town market would be. As the village got closer, he noticed that the houses were wooden, with thatched roofs. During the time he had been walking towards the village, he had tried to avoid looking at one building in particular — the grandest one of them all, at the very end, standing on a small hill. An old church, of red and white. A somewhat familiar, yet unwelcome sight for Jannus.

'And who is our vaunted visitor?' a warm voice spoke out from the house to the left of him.

Jannus turned quickly, and moved a few steps backwards. Out of the house walked a woman, clad in old-style robes, coloured amethyst, yet frayed at the edges, as if some wild beast had once clawed at them. The woman walked gracefully toward Jannus, and kept her eyes focused on him. A rope belt was tied around the woman's waist, and connected to the rope, Jannus could see two small figures, on opposite sides of the knot, in the middle as if in equipoise: a fable-like animal of diverse origins, and a humanoid creature, with spear and shield in hand. The woman now stood a few feet in front of him. She had long hair, a silvery grey, a golden ornament cresting her brow; amethyst stones glittered amidst the gold, making the woman almost the only source of light in this otherwise empty town, other than the small glimpse of light in the distant sky.

Jannus looked at her face. He thought he saw just a hint of a smile. But he could not be sure. Part of him wanted to run away. Part of him wondered if he should kneel to the woman. A silly notion, he knew, yet the figure in front of him looked royal in a way he could not explain. He had not grown up in a country with royalty, and felt no particular sense of deference or allegiance. Still, the notion was there.

'You have not answered my question, good sir,' the woman said to him, not unkindly. Jannus was uncertain what to say, or even if he should say anything at all. He had forgotten the rules here. Should he speak? He decided against his immediate instinct, and to engage.

'I'm Jannus,' he managed. And he looked at her. And kept looking. *Apparently, I'm not my usual self this night,* he thought, irritated. *"Jan, the ultimate wordsmith, he of great renown!"* The woman in front of him had kept looking at him, apparently patiently, giving him time to comport himself. *Maybe she is used to these kinds of situations,* he thought, with some amusement, starting to relax somewhat.

'I'm not sure where I am,' he said to the woman. 'I'm not sure I'm supposed to be here.'

Jannus looked around the village, still empty beyond the two of them, standing in front of the house in the middle of the only road. The house to the right of them kept shifting in and out of existence, sometimes coming back with the doorway in a different placement, other times with only a bare wall, before shifting back to its original appearance. He looked back at her.

'And I'm afraid I don't know you either, my lady.' *Lady?* he thought, bemused. *Lady? Where did that come from?*

The lady in question had nodded regally at his answer though, and gave him a slight smile in appreciation.

'Ah, a visitor in truth then,' she said. Jannus noticed that the woman had a strange ability to look at him, while simultaneously looking to be gazing just at something slightly beyond him. 'Most visitors look just as you do, bewildered and unsure of themselves. Most leave here quickly, leaving our lands before we can converse.'

Jannus tried to make sense of what the lady had just said, while trying to find a way to keep the conversation going. Again, to his own vast surprise, he found that he indeed was inclined to "converse".

'There have been others here, my lady?'

The woman did not answer or affirm immediately. Instead, she pointed to the biggest building in the village, other than the red and white church.

'There, we all used to gather, to meet and converse. We were many here, once upon a time. Most are lost now.' Jannus thought he detected a sadness of great profundity there, yet he did not want to interrupt. 'All that remains now is this valley of pain you see before you, the eternal desolation, on this sad shore.'

Jannus found himself mesmerised by the woman's words. And mystified. Suddenly, he did not want the dreamscape to end; he wanted to learn more about this whole thing.

'Are you alone here, my lady?' he asked her.

This time, she laughed softly. 'No, you are here, are you not, good sir?'

He smiled at that. 'I guess so.'

Mielle seemed to consider for a moment, before speaking. When she did, Jannus thought her tone had changed just a bit, and her stance had also shifted to seem a bit more relaxed. *Maybe she's getting used to it,* Jannus wondered.

'In truth, I am the last colourless soul here, good sir. The last to sing our broken songs, and the last to greet a friendly visitor. I am called Mielle.'

To Jannus, she still looked to be of regal nature, yet her demeanour and her words had now told him otherwise. Whoever this woman was (or had been), he thought her to be more of a diplomat, or a guide of sorts.

'Well, it's nice to meet you, Mielle,' he said, mindful of his manners. 'I'm called Jannus. But I'm not sure what I'm doing here, myself,' he added, sheepishly. 'I don't quite know how I'm supposed to help you here'.

He told her of the impossible, or rather, *illogical,* things he had already witnessed; things that kept changing, or did not make any immediate sense. She titled her head slightly, as if wanting to get a better view of him.

'The nature of these places is mostly unknown, Jannus. Sometimes things are the way we expect, and sometimes they are not.'

Jannus, forgetting his manners again, gave an exasperated sigh. 'Well, that's not exactly reassuring, my lady'. He spun around to see if he could catch anything around that defied his expectation, or seemed out of the ordinary. Somewhat disappointed, Jannus found nothing obvious around him changing, or senseless. He looked back at her. 'As I said, I'm not sure how I'm supposed to help you; I seem quite lost myself.'

For the first time since they met in this empty dream-village, she smiled at him, fully. 'Ah Jan, even a man in his best age is only dust.' And with those words, she started to fade, became translucent, and then disappeared, beyond his sight.

'Mielle?' he called out. 'Mielle?'

The village was once again empty, until the purple shadow slowly darkened, and he fell into sleep even more deeply before he would wake up.

The next morning, Jannus was irritated at himself. For once, he got out of bed quickly, washed his face and brushed his teeth, and opened up the living-room door to the backyard, and the kitchen window, just to get some fresh air into the house. Even though he had got rid of all the dirty dishes and all the bottles more than a week ago, the air in the house was still somewhat tainted by the leftover smell. It was difficult to get rid of that smell of beer and wine, especially if you had been going for a couple of days. It seemed to stick to your skin and your clothes. Part of that had to do with the fact that you tended not to wash or clean either, if you had been drinking for two days. But Jannus thought he had removed most of the taint from his liquid addictions.

Not all of the bottles though; only the empty ones on the floor and the surfaces. Not the ones hidden in the closets, away from sight yet never completely out of mind. He had learned that from the best, after all. His mother had exerted herself greatly at hiding stuff like that. Jannus would never have considered her creative, yet her ability to veil her addictions without compunctions had been something to admire, and eventually, emulate. Not that he had meant to, of course. Jannus could still recall how he would sometimes try to hug her, seeing if he could smell the wine on her. Never beer or any other type of beverage. Wine had been her drink of choice, her solace, her secret that everybody knew yet never once spoke about. Not directly, anyway. Whenever he had given her such an embrace, there had always been a short moment, a glimpse of doubt in her features. But quickly that had turned to her standard, general look of complacency.

Jannus had tried his best to break the pattern. Yet in this one thing he was almost like a mirror image of his mother. In fact, he thought he had become even better at it than her. As he was waiting for the morning brew to be ready, Jannus turned on the radio. Not to listen to any specific programme or genre, really, but just to have some background noise, something to fill out the silence. Also, to get his mind off the hidden treasures in the closets. His current annoyance this morning came from last night's dreamscape; both at the rather abrupt ending to the whole thing, but also at his own demeanour and actions throughout. He had hardly asked Mielle any questions. Questions, regarding who she was, what *she* was doing there, what was the name of the village, and so on. Just after waking up he had thought to write down all his questions for the next time; then he had sheepishly realised that he most likely would not be able to bring the questions with him, *into* the dream! And Jannus was not sure of the level of agency he would have in any case: was it like a normal dream where things just seemed to happen randomly, most of the time? Or could he actually *choose* where to go? And would he end up the same place the next time? And would the lady of last night's dream reappear? Surprised, he found himself wishing that would be so. The most peculiar thing about her had been the way she was dressed, and her way of speech. It seemed old, somehow. *Archaic,* even. That *could* have been the nature of the dream, naturally.

And it was funny how the dream took place near the waters: Jannus had never had any sort of proclivity toward a body of large water. His grandmother had told him much of his grandfather, long since deceased before Jannus had the chance to meet him. 'Oh, how he had liked to take your father fishing, when he was a boy,' she had told him more than once, when Jannus himself had been a boy. *Betila* was the name of his boat, not fit for the great seas, but great for travelling rivers and fjords. It had been named for Jannus' father, and his two siblings, now estranged for many years. Jannus' grandfather had taken the first two letters of each of their names, and put them together. Quite ingeniously, admittedly. The grand-pater old man had been a sailor in his younger years. Though his grandmother had told much, Jannus had never heard the full story, but Jannus knew that something had happened to his father, when he had been a teenage boy himself. His grandmother had been reticent in speaking about those events for some reason. But Jannus had surmised that it had something to do with his late grandfather, of whom his grandmother had spoken mostly in glorious terms. His father had never spoken much of those fishing trips, only hinted at them, when he had had too much to drink.

'Your father has quite a temper on him,' his grandmother had consoled him after another occasion. 'It's always been that way with him.'

Jannus knew that his father had not spoken to his own father for a very long time before the latter passed away. For many years Jannus had just assumed that the two of them had been in a fight of sorts, for whatever reason, and that his father had been sent away from home to travel the world on the seas. When he had first heard that story, he thought of it as an adventure; great sails fluttering, wood creaking, waves crashing, while his father had seen the wide world unfold before him.

Later on, he had realised it had probably been everything but adventurous. And he could certainly remember his temper. Though out on the boat, out there in the fjord, his father had seemed different. A calmer, more temperate sort of man. *At peace.* Jannus supposed he should have been more appreciative of those times, yet he had been nervous of the water, of falling in, and drowning, and getting lost in the deep below. He had read stories of such things, and he knew it could also happen to him.

As he poured his morning coffee, and took a sip of the almost still-boiling water, he looked at the front page of yesterday's paper. Jannus noticed, with some amusement, that he had apparently left some evidence of the last time he had looked at it; a coffee-coloured circle from the bottom of his mug was encircling part of a headline about some sort of tragedy or controversy. Usually, he only glanced at the front page, knowing that if any substance was to be found, it would be found within, sometimes hidden away in some forgotten corner of the newspaper; in some place that usually would not garner the first few points of attention. His own doctor had even advised him not to follow the news that much.

'There is a lot going on world, right now, Mr Rubens,' he had told him. 'And not all of it is going to lift your spirits, you know what I mean?'

Jannus had agreed, since he found that agreeing got him the medication quicker. He knew that the doctor had been right, of course. When you were in a state of mental imbalance, you would usually react to certain events in a more negative way, or it could have a greater impact on you than it usually would have. So, an overexposure to all things negative, such as a great deal of the news in the world tended to be, could affect him badly.

'Now, I know you know this, Mr Rubens,' his

doctor had added, just before Jannus had left him, prescription safely secured. 'But I think you need to get out more, you know? Get out and meet some people, maybe. Or just take a short walk outside every day, even though you'll probably not feel like it.'

The advice had been well meant, Jannus knew. For the first few months after that visit to the doctor's, he had not adhered to it, though. He had kept to the shadows of his house and his mind and his heart. Yet slowly, he had progressed to the point where he would go outside for a walk, once a week. Sometimes even two. So, things were progressing, all things considered.

Jannus had quite the ambivalent relationship to his doctor. These last couple of years, Jannus had felt meek and obedient every time he walked into the clinic, almost subservient. It had not always been so; before his fall, he had rarely been to the doctor's, preferring and relying on his own counsel, and expertise. And when he finally *did* go (under much pressure from his former wife), it was as if he and his doctor were engaged in a sort of tarantella; in constant competition trying to upstage the other guy in the room. At least, Jannus had had that experience.

He kept turning the pages of the newspaper, not really reading or absorbing or reflecting, being preoccupied with his own musings, as he so often was.

When you were down, you should cherish even the objectively smallest efforts; for an individual who feels down most things can feel like a trial, or climbing a mountaintop, on the wrong day. Jannus knew this could be difficult to perceive for someone who had not been in that place. And even if you had tried something similar, the experience would still be different. While turning the pages of the newspaper, skimming through controversy after tragedy described in less than salubrious detail, the former therapist thought back to one of his former clients. Or rather, two of his former clients. Twin girls, aged eight or nine. He had been commissioned by the local trauma centre to perform crisis treatment for some of the people involved. A ship had crashed into the rocky shore, or maybe it hit an iceberg. The immediate reports had been confusing, as they sometimes would be during crisis. Nothing new there. What was known was that a big group of people had been involved in that particular tragedy; the people on the ship, naturally, but also people on land witnessing the whole thing unfold. Not to mention family and friends, and the community as a whole. Jannus had not been the only therapist involved; a lot of personnel had been summoned to aid the local community: therapists, healthcare workers, social workers, and so on.

Jannus could not recall a whole lot from that day; most of it was blurred and hazy. A lot of the stories were very similar, as per the common event they had all been a part of. But the memory of the twins had remained with him. Maybe because it was sort of unrelated to the main event. Or at least, their experience could not be directly tied to it.

The twins' father had gone out in his small fishing boat that morning, never to return. The family man, the father of two, never reappeared, and the two girls had waited by the shore for him to come back. As Jannus had understood it, the family had been well-known in the local community, and the local social services. The family did not have a lot, financially, and they often relied on the father and how much he would gather from his fishing boat. That very morning, when the great ship had crashed, he had made one last journey.

The two girls had reacted very differently, even though they both had lost a father that day. One of them had been very talkative, almost chatty, as if unaffected by the events that had just transpired. Maybe she had not quite understood yet, or maybe her child-mind had protected itself, shielded off that part of the mind that was not yet ready to process what had happened in her life. The other one was very quiet in her demeanour, almost catatonic. She gave only one-word answers, and sometimes not even that. Just a shrug of the shoulders, or shaking her head. Strangely enough, Jannus had been more worried about the talkative twin, at least in terms of the possible long-term consequences.

No one had ever found out what exactly had happened to their father, as far as Jannus knew. They never found his body. Jannus was aware that this sometimes happened, particularly in isolated communities. Someone would leave on an errand of some sort and never return. Whether they had left of their own volition and motivation, or if something tragic or criminal had happened to them, were questions often left for their families and friends. Jannus had left them that day, knowing that part of them would always live with the vain hope of him returning in his small fishing boat. As a therapist it was difficult to know why some clients' stories touched you personally, and others did not. Two similar stories or issues from two different clients could evoke quite different reactions. Jannus thought it had to do with a lot of factors intertwining; the relationship between client and therapist, for one, but also, what you had experienced in your own life, and your current life situation, and general health. Not that it should be considered a negative thing to have experienced trials in life yourself. Yet he did consider it beneficial to have resolved those issues in large part, before deciding to help other people with similar challenges.

Jannus had finally turned the last page of the newspaper, without really reading any of it in depth. The last page was reserved for local news. Apparently, there was quite the debate of where to build a third connection to alleviate the local traffic. Arguments went back and forth regarding where it would be most beneficial and least detrimental. Jannus had almost no interest in these concerns; the road before him was not inconsequential, yet it remained a lonely one.

Chapter V

A Wicked Mind

Blood on the snowy ground, ice-picks falling from the roof's edge, cracking in two, hitting the ground. A chained dog, a man in shades, whipped dog, chained to the ground.

The last remnants of last night's dreamscape, with its disturbing images, were still churning in Jannus' mind as he was pushing the shopping cart around in the local grocery store. He usually went early in the morning, when few people were shopping; mostly the elderly, and young people from the local trade school, when they were on their break. Jannus had never liked shopping; most of the time he planned whatever it was he would buy, and even made a mental map of how he would proceed in the store to make his visit the most efficient, and short.

He was standing in the fruit section, when he suddenly heard someone talk to him; an elderly man, was standing on the opposite site of the aisle. In one gnarled hand, he held an equally wrinkled apple, with brown spots on one side, and in the other hand, also gnarled, he held what looked to be a somewhat fresh pear.

'Excuse me?' Jannus said. He had noticed, that he started every other conversation with these words, having not heard the preamble, being too preoccupied with inner turmoil. The old man was wearing a marine-blue trench coat, and a scarf around his neck, with a classic, English, square pattern. A great mane of white hair was combed back from his brow. He looked quite stylish actually, as he looked from apple to pear, from hand to hand, to Jannus, and back again.

'Can you believe this?' the old man repeated with a smile. Jannus looked from fruit to fruit, somewhat confused. He was looking for oranges, himself. Maybe his bafflement was apparent, since the old man elaborated. 'Can you believe they still put these bad fruits in with the good ones? Don't they know it's bad for the good fruit?' The old man's smile and twinkle in his eyes took the edge off his words.

Jannus truly did not wish to engage himself in any conversation in any store, yet he found himself softening to the old man's demeanour. He often found himself more receptive to the elderly, when compared to people his own age, or younger.

'I'm sure they know of it, sir,' he said to the old man, while picking out the best-looking oranges, and putting them into a brown paper bag.

'Well, they didn't get this one, you see,' the old man lamented, and turned the apple around, as if making sure Jannus could get a clear view of the clearly not-up-to-standard fruit. Jannus looked into the brown-paper bag in his shopping cart. He had suddenly lost count of how many oranges he had gathered. There was an offer for ten oranges at a reduced price. He still had three more to go, by the looks of it.

The old man was still holding one piece of fruit in each hand, as if unsure of how to proceed. Jannus was ready to move on to the next purchase, yet something made him hesitate about leaving the old man bewildered.

'Maybe you could just leave it at the front, so people can see it's a bad one?' he suggested. The old man was already smiling, yet it seemed his face lit up even more at the offered solution.

'Yes, Yes! I can do that. Surely, I can do that!' He put the fruit back, turned it a couple of times, and then took another one, more fresh-looking.

Nodding, and just a tiny bit satisfied that he had somehow been helpful to another human being, Jannus prepared to leave. He stopped when the old man started talking again. Not directly to Jannus this time; it was more akin to the way people talk when they have been alone for a while; halfway between talking to yourself and to someone who is no longer there.

'Ah, I remember the first time I bit into an apple. They had just got a new shipment at the docks, and Father and I were one of the first ones on the spot to get ourself a whole basket of the things!' the old man laughed softly, and sadly. 'Ah, I had never had anything like it, son,' he said, while he looked down into his own shopping cart.

Jannus noticed that the old man's hands were huge, and a bit scarred, as if he had had a lifetime of hard labour. They were shaking just a bit: if that was just an old-age thing, or if the elderly man was just moved by his own memories, Jannus did not know. But the old man had spoken of his experience as if it had been almost spiritual. He could imagine the old man as just a boy, blissfully taking his first bite of an apple. Jannus did not think any sort of food experience was special or spiritual in any way. Sure, he had his favourite foods, and even favourites he used to like to prepare. But mostly, it was just a means to an end, a necessity. For a second, Jannus wondered if he should change his perspective on the matter, but then, just as quickly, decided that he most likely would not.

'My wife preferred pears, you know?' the old man said suddenly, as he took another one from the pile. 'I don't really like the taste of them myself; they're either too sweet or too spicy or too tangy, never a balance between one of them!' The old man seemed to be picking up speed as he talked, though he sounded sad at the same time. He looked at the fruit a bit more while turning it around in his hand. Then he shifted his gaze to Jannus. 'I usually buy one or two, and eat them anyway. For my wife, you see.'

Jannus understood. 'I'm sorry,' he commiserated.

The old man gave a short nod in answer, so Jannus

decided it was safe enough to leave him there with his apples and pears and memories.

On the way home from the grocery store, Jannus walked through the Garden; not because of the scenery, necessarily, but because there were fewer people there, in the early-morning hours. Outside the park the morning traffic would dominate the soundscape of the day, disturbing his inner peace, such as it was. And he still preferred to avoid as many people as possible. Walking through the park it was easier to hide, and disengage.

Not that he believed other people were out to hurt him directly, or harboured malevolent intentions toward him; *most* people that Jannus had met throughout his life had been good people, kind-hearted, and well-intentioned. During his career he had spent a few years working with clients who were, at the time, incarcerated. And he had found, to his own surprise, that he had been able to empathise with the majority of them, despite their actions in life. He would never be able to sympathise or condone the actions themselves. But he *could* acknowledge the people they had once been, and all the various things that had brought them to their current predicament.

Jannus had to change his course on the dirt path along the small lake; some of the bushes almost reached the whole way across. He knew that a private company had the responsibility of maintaining the park premises, which included (ideally) keeping the place clean and approachable for everyone. Apparently, someone had been somewhat lax in their duties. With two brown grocery bags in his arms, he walked carefully through the small passage he was allowed, touching neither leaf nor water. After that, there was only a short walk to the southern exit from the park.

When he got home, relieved that he had been unapproached (one had been enough), his thoughts strayed to old Mrs Kearney next door. Jannus had not seen her for a few days, which was somewhat unusual; usually he could catch a glimpse of her taking a walk. She and her late husband had been quite the active seniors. They had never talked every other day, since Jannus had been so eager and successful in his avoidant behaviours.

Not that he was worried. The last time he had seen her through his kitchen window, she was taking a walk outside with a younger woman (who still looked older than himself), whom he presumed was her daughter. And the day before that, she had knocked on his door, offering some homemade cooking (Irish stew), which Jannus gratefully accepted. Most of the food he ate these days was not of his own produce or own making; for the most part it was canned or prepared. While he filled up his refrigerator, fridge and kitchen cupboards with new supplies for the next week (again, mostly canned or prepared foods), Jannus thought of the notion that he should perhaps introduce Mrs Kearney and the old man from the grocery store. Quickly, he abandoned the idea;

on the one hand, they might have a lot to talk about, and share, due to their similar experiences. However, it was most likely too soon for Mrs Kearney, having just lost her life-partner. And lastly, Jannus did not think of himself as a good mediator. Not any more.

He took one of the oranges from the bag, and cut it up into four pieces, leaving the peel on, like his grandmother used to prepare them for consumption. He put them on a breakfast plate, and went into the living room. Except for his couch, a coffee table, the television with its stand, and the corner cupboard, the living room was pretty sparse. Only a single painting hung on the household-white wall — an unnamed landscape-scenery in colours of green, and brown and blue. A hilly area with a single house halfway to the summit, the sea visible in the distance.

While he lay on the couch, listening to the gentle sounds from the open backyard-door, Jannus thought once again of his former work-life.

'You must find something in people that you can understand,' he had once learned. 'If you cannot, that client may not be for you; worst case, you should recommend another therapist, and bring the sessions to a close,' one of his old professors had once lectured. Jannus could not recall his name, only that he had once worked as a clinical psychologist, who, by the time Jannus was a student, had concerned himself more with teaching.

Maybe last night's dreamscape had reminded him

of one such closure: a client, with whom Jannus had held only two sessions, including the introductory one. That particular client had disturbed Jannus in a way he could not fully explain, and that he could not manage in a professional manner; at least not that early in his career. The client had been a man in his early twenties, only a few years younger than Jannus himself at that time, in truth. He had spoken of retribution; he had spoken of vengeance. He had revealed fantasies of flame and shadow. He had spoken of his dark, burning heart and of crumbling nations; of how the world was a place of pain, a world that had put every kind of hurt upon him. And he had divulged his plans for the future, for the world of no-tomorrow, and how things should be done. Jannus had noticed how the client had used strange, archaic references that Jannus had to look up to understand. And even then, it had mostly been a matter of interpretation. The client could have meant something else entirely, or just led Jannus astray, through a wild hunt through the dark. And most disturbingly, he had spoken of all of this with almost no asperity; just a calm, relaxed, almost polite manner.

The man had been so detailed in his descriptions that Jannus had been deeply concerned, even after only two sessions. He could easily imagine that his client, one day, would be caught in flagrante delicto; for a few days, Jannus had even pictured himself as the man's first victim of retribution, before his former wife had calmed him down. Yet the whole thing had proven to be too intolerable in terms of keeping the therapeutic alliance alive. It had been easy enough to inform the client of the decision, that one of Jannus' colleagues would take over the sessions. Jannus did not think that the client had expected it necessarily, but judging by the man's health journal, Jannus had not been the first therapist, not by quite a margin. Yet one thing still remained with him after all these days. Right before the client had left the room for the last time, he had spoken about something quite profound to Jannus, something that had made him somewhat distrait for a while. The soon-to-be-former-client had said to his soon-to-be-former therapist, that he had always wanted to make an impact; not that he wanted to stand out front and centre, getting all the attention and praise; but something more akin to playing an obligatory part, essential to the piece as a whole, and something that would make a difference if it was absent. That was all. *That* had been somewhat understandable to Jannus, which he had also found disconcerting. At the time Jannus had been afraid that by understanding this particular client, that he was also somewhat *like* the client. One last peculiar quirk of the client, that Jannus could recall, was that he had a habit of giving himself odd titles, or strange (to Jannus at least) self-references, almost as though he had spoken of someone else, or maybe an alternate persona of some sort. Jannus' thoughts quickly went between these words and the envelope now placed on the kitchen counter.

He suddenly had a bitter taste in his mouth; accidently he had bitten into the orange peel. He sat up in the couch. 'Be careful not to eat the peel, Jan,' his grandmother had once advised him, yet it seemed he that forgotten that piece of information. After a bit of spitting and cursing, Jannus took the last piece of orange, removed the peel carefully, and devoured it whole.

And the gentleman in shadows looked on, while he waited still. Waited, with a longed-for smile, still held by love, long unrewarded. 'Ah, sing your song for me, if you'd please, dear Caina awaits me,' the gentleman spoke gently, while he rocked back and forth. He had waited long, too long, much too long, here in the shadows, kept in the dark like a dog in chains, forever rooted. Kept in place, when the sun surely blazed outside, keeping people happy and warm. 'Not I,' he demurred. 'I will wait for you no longer.'

Chapter VI

Recyclable Echoes

Self-denial was a curious thing, Jannus knew. He had met the phenomena in other people, as well as in himself. He had often wondered if it was an inborn ability, or something you learned along the way. As he turned off the television, he reflected on how difficult it was for everyone across the board to keep to their vaunted values, especially in tough times where you had to endure hardships, when it all was put to the test.

There had been another dream last night. They were becoming much more frequent: it was almost every other night at this point. This meant that Jannus woke up, exhausted, every other morning, after having a dreamscape experience. Apparently, the visions came with a certain price, and took their toll. And due to him being in the beginnings of a recovery phase with limited resources, whether mental or emotional, the toll was more extensive. And mostly unwelcome.

In last night's dreamscape, the lady Mielle had looked more dishevelled in her robes. She had spoken of 'lives undiscerning with light spread in unequal measure,' and of some sort of discord which had assailed their already divided city'. That did not make a lot of sense to Jannus, but Mielle had fallen silent after that, apparently not willing to elaborate on her statements.

She *had*, however, told him a story about a hero, as far as Jannus had surmised, though Mielle had never named him as such. *And he went forward, fire blazing from his brow. And the people followed him without question, transfixed by his gaze, and his words. His blazon showed a great, golden war horn, on crimson cloth. And as it fluttered with every gust of wind, we travelled in his wake to whatever destination he chose. At last, we came to a great plain, where his plan became clear; an opposing army, clad in righteous blue and majestic silver. And as the daystar shone above, oh how they glittered! As they drew their weapons, fear took hold of us, hooks sinking deep. And we looked to our lord, who seemed unmoved, and steadfast. For a moment, we still feared, but then he laughed and laughed, and drew a weapon of his own. A great warhammer of heavy burden that only he could wield, in his right hand. And in his left, an equally great tower shield, red and gold. And as he stood there, he was an answer, a solution to what was before us, and what we had left behind. Our fear evaporated as we laughed alongside our lord, and then we ran and then we screamed, peasant spears in hand. And as we ran towards our moment most glorious, we did not see the ground crumble underneath.*

After he had felt the dreamscape evaporate, he had heard her whisper, 'Under the auspices of the great warlord, we continued our losing struggles to no avail'. Jannus had the sensation that he was not meant to hear those final whispered words. As for her story, he had been enraptured, though he did not understand its specific meanings, or why Mielle had chosen to tell him. After the visions stopped, there had followed a collection of dreams that had seemed more real, and natural. Three pictures on the wall at Grandmother's, the wall painted lime-green, now faded with time. A dining room table filled with all manner of pastries. One of the photographs depicted his grandmother (looking kind) and his grandfather (looking austere), a tradition-bound man, according to his grandmother. After these more regular dreams, Jannus never felt exhausted afterwards, only reminiscent.

As Jannus was preparing his morning coffee (untraditionally with sugar, for extra energy), he reflected on some of his former clients. He could not escape the thought that the letter was from one of them. He had excluded family and friends from the equation. He could not see what kind of motivation any of them would have. Colleagues? No. He had always been quite stalwart in terms of keeping his professional and private life separate. Almost draconically so. He knew that some of his former co-workers thought this cold and cynical, but Jannus actually thought it was the most thoughtful thing to do for everyone involved. His former wife? That did not compute either; to her undeniable credit, she had always been very direct with whatever she wanted of him. Moving into the living-room to get to the backyard, Jannus took a sip of his coffee, and grimaced. Too sweet, even with one spoonful.

It was a beautiful morning outside. It had rained slightly during the night, so the grass was wet, and the air, fresh and crisp. The skies were only lightly clouded, and as the sun was already peering through, Jannus judged that the day would be much warmer by midday.

His thoughts wandered back to the letter, and whoever might be the possible culprit. He did not often think of his sister, estranged as they had been for many years; they had been quite close as children, but somewhere along the way they had separated. There had not been a definite argument or an unsolvable conflict of any sort: they had just drifted apart over time, being busy with their own lives. Once, that had been a source of sadness, something regretful, but by now it was somewhat of a rarity if he even thought of her. And he supposed, it was the same for her. Jannus considered it a normal thing in life that you would meet a lot of people on your way, who, for one reason or another, you would never meet again, or with whom you'd somehow fail to maintain a consistent relationship. And so it had been with his sister.

Concerning former clients, Jannus thought back to the time when he had visited a school. He had been working as a counsellor for day-cares and public schools. The school in question had been worried about a certain girl, in the sixth grade: she never spoke in class, and she seemed isolated, socially, from the rest of the class. Her teachers did not suspect the girl was being bullied, nor that she was decidedly unpopular. Still, they remained worried that her development was perhaps not as it should be.

Jannus had met the girl, along with her father, in an unoccupied classroom on the school premises. The girl had, at first, seemed shy and unresponsive. Her long, ash-brown hair had been covering most of her face, as she kept looking down, answering mostly with short sharp nods, and by shrugging her shoulders. When the girl had tried to talk with him, Jannus discovered that the girl had a very pronounced stutter. He knew a bit about this particular challenge; in some literature, it was called 'the invisible handicap', though other handicaps and pathologies shared this distinction. Every other syllable (vowels in particular) was accompanied by a violent backward jerk of the head. Jannus had learned that these symptoms were 'secondary', a mostly physical symptom, that the stutter developed to avoid the actual stuttering. Usually, what ended up happening, though, was that the secondary symptom was even more apparent than the stuttering itself. Which was, to be sure, the very opposite of the intended effect.

The girl preferred to keep her silence; when she did not talk, no one could see what she wanted to hide.

Jannus had discovered, early on, that the girl had actually been quite clever. Very much so, in fact. Which could also be seen in the fact that her written assignments were graded much higher than her oral ones. As such, there was a clear delineation concerning her challenges. In the visit, one teacher had even described her as 'impertinent'. That had made Jannus angry, he remembered, as he took another sip of the too-sweet morning coffee, the first few rays of the daystar making their appearance. During the visit, there was no mention of the girl's stuttering issues, though of course the teachers had known. Why would they not have? Disinterest or impoliteness was not the issue at hand, whenever the girl had not answered directly during class.

'The people you collaborate with in your field of work will not always show verisimilitude', his old clinical psychology professor had once told him. 'Not necessarily because of ill intent, Jannus: some people might not know better through no fault of their own.' Jannus still did not know if he agreed with that sentiment; it had been difficult to recall at times. He had not always shown the proper patience and delectation in the people he had worked with, the former therapist now knew, especially when faced with any shade of deprecation. Even at the end, just before his fall, the sight of birds of prey in their merciless hunt against unsuspecting victims could still provoke a *re*action in him, if not exactly an *action.*

Outside, it looked to be a day with fine weather. Just yesterday, he had woken up to a dark and grey day, the morning mist covering most things just beyond the backyard. The streetlights had looked like ghost lights, their faint emanations guiding people through the grey and white. Suddenly he noticed something out of the ordinary; another white envelope was sticking out of the mailbox. Jannus sighed, and put down his coffee mug, a little too violently. Getting the key just beside the front door, he went outside with a strange foreboding of what he would find. Inside the mailbox, he found another envelope, similar to the first one, though this one seemed a bit lighter, or thinner, at least. Beyond that, the box was almost full of leaflets and circulars. A few even fell out when Jannus opened it. He cursed, and bent down to retrieve them. While doing so, he looked up to check the mailbox; he still had one of those stickers you had to get, so the paperboy would not deliver to you. *And he always brings more,* he thought, amusing himself. Jannus noticed that his particular sticker's expiration date was last year. For some reason you had to update your sticker, every second year or so. When he had gathered all of them, he went inside, leaflets and circulars in one hand, and the envelope in the other; part of him did not want to let the envelope get lost in the mix.

Jannus left all the leaflets and circulars on the living-room table. Most likely he would never read them; at most, he would glance through the local circulars for his weekly visit to the grocery store.

His main motivation, right at this moment, though, was the envelope, and whatever he would find within. This time it was only a single A4 page, written in a similar hand to the first one, yet slightly different. As if someone had tried to imitate his own style of writing. It took only a few seconds to read the single page of content; the wording was relatively simple and direct.

Dear Mr Rubens, psychologist sublime, have you still no notion, still no idea of what is to come?

Can you fathom the reckoning that soon will be brought to bear? Did you ever realise the hurt you wrought?

The pain you delivered? Come to me here in the dark, where I'll wait for you.

Come soon, my dear. Come to me, and stay.

Love beckons you home, and there you will see.

Jannus' whole body shook when he had finished reading. He glanced briefly at the cupboard with the liquid treasure inside, but quickly pushed that temptation aside. In the bottom-right corner of the page was noted the same address as had been written in the first letter, this time in a much more forceful, almost aggressive hand. Still, he had no idea of who the sender was. Almost. Some of the wording seemed familiar somehow. It seemed aggressive and demanding, and mocking, in a way. Yet Jannus also detected a degree of ambivalence in the language used, as if the sender also was in need of attention. *Acceptance,* even. Or maybe that was just his imagination.

Unlike the first letter, this one seemed to have a bigger effect on him. The first one made him worried, sure, but also curious, while this letter made him fearful, as if the stakes were somehow higher this time around. As if his time was running out. As ever, when consequence ever reared its demonic head, Jannus' first instinct was to flee, to get away. He had done so in his personal life, as well as in his professional life, many a time. He walked back and forth in front of the television in the living-room, still with the letter in hand, the sunny day outside forgotten for the moment.

Most of all he wanted to ignore this whole thing; maybe it was an ill-conceived prank. A fragment of his consciousness even had the silly notion that this was a mistake; maybe he was not meant to be the receiver. But if so, it would have been a double-mistake, since this was the second letter, and in this letter, unlike the first one, he was named. So Jannus could not accept that explanation, however much he would have liked. No, this whole thing was definitely about him, and someone who wanted something from him. It seemed like no matter how much he tried to run away from that, it would always find him again. He crushed the letter in his fist, as the day began to darken again.

CHAPTER VII

Follow the Push and Pull

The regal voice of Mielle still echoed in his ears, as he woke up a few days later. 'We were perilously close to the infinite night. There had been an intemperate soul among us; a serpent spirit that had felt ever denied. And we were too late. Too late.' And a few flickering images remained as well: a disconsolate family leaving the shore-lands in a snowstorm, the winds almost contemptuously ripping the adults and children apart. Jannus had feared for their safety and survival, seeing the steady ascent ahead of them. They had seemed desperate and tired, yet they had kept running.

Refraining from the morning coffee, he quickly put on his boots and jacket, and walked outside. He was heading for the Garden, and he wanted to take a few walks around the small lake today as a morning exercise, but also because these walks served as a good motivator for reflection. Though the weather report promised this would be another sunny day, locally the morning air was still quite cool. Not only were the ducks out this morning (a few ducklings were still asleep, some of them only with one eye open, when Jannus passed them by), but he also saw other kinds of avian wildlife that he could not immediately recognise. There were black birds with little red marks just above the beak, and he even saw a few birds standing on one leg on small stones in the shallow water. He did not know their name, either. None of the avian life paid him much attention; he was always careful when he walked here, not wanting to disturb or upset any of the natural life. Jannus made sure to keep a few feet distant to any wildlife he was cognisant of. Whenever he *was* cognisant, naturally!

He was quite absorbed with his own inner turmoil and difficulty of deciding what to do. Jannus would never describe himself as a searchlight soul. He was a man of pride who wanted to take care of his own life, and issues; fastidious to a fault. As he made care not to step on a duckling walking self-importantly across the dirt path, he smiled wryly. *A family tradition, at this point; a prideful man walking his own path unmindful of everyone but himself.*

Sometimes he just wanted to abstain from all of it, retreat from whatever this mortal, modern life entailed. What was the river of forgetfulness called again? Styx? Lethe? He could not recall. Whatever it was, Jannus just wanted to rest his head there, at the shore. The thoughts of another former client of his intruded upon his mind, as he came back to his starting point at the southern exit, and started yet another round around the lake. The client in question was a woman in her mid-thirties. She had struggled mightily with intrusive thoughts and ritualistic behaviour. Not responding to the intrusive thoughts — that was to say, *acting* upon them — would result in emotional and physical suffering. The prime ritual was washing her hands, the thoughts many and varied, yet always catastrophic in nature. Always portraying the worst-case scenario of what would most likely happen if she did not succumb to whatever the scenario was that day. The sessions had been very successful in terms of the woman reaching her therapeutic goals. Yet it had been one of those cases where the social issues were so prominent. As such, the same day that Jannus and the client had finished their objectively and subjectively successful session-work, the woman had been thrown out of her apartment, having no immediate place to go, being estranged from most of her familial relationships.

Jannus felt himself tiring; this time, he caught the self-chastising thoughts and let them disperse. As he found the nearest bench, he felt quite satisfied. Though he was quite adept in terms of understanding and dealing with negative automatic thinking, he was the consummate proof that a therapist was immune to their possible derogatory effect. These past few years he had found himself caught up in their whirlwind more often than not. One particular client had described them (after Jannus had provided the theoretical concept) as "spider webs", which Jannus had found an even better description; it was as if you had become stuck in a pattern which ever expanded, not daring to move or make a noise. Either you would risk getting stuck on something else, or something dangerous would notice and approach.

Jannus was still debating whether to leave his home for the address written on both letters. He had also debated whether or not he should contact the local authorities about the whole thing, but had discarded the idea. Jannus had a bit of a history with the local authorities. Sometimes, during a drinking bout, he would make a mess of things. Alcohol, specifically the darker liqueurs, tended to have a debilitating effect on his personality. Or rather, seemed to *enhance* the darker parts of his personality. Just a few months ago, he had — for some odd reason — decided to go to the hardware store, the next city over. And his temper had got the better of him, and he had started yelling at the people there (personnel and customers, both) with such great impudicity that the personnel had called the police. Luckily, he had not visited the *local* hardware store, but it was within the same municipality, and as a consequence, also the same local authorities he had to deal with. And the incident at the hardware store had not been of a singular nature, these past few years. So, they knew Jannus quite well, and he had absolutely no inclination to reacquaint himself with them any sooner than he had to.

Jannus did recognise that there was a certain strangeness to it all. But so far, the embarrassment he would likely suffer by going to the local authorities had proved to be the greater. So far. And again, he could not find any explicit threat in either letter; in his view, none of the wording seemed to adumbrate or portent any kind of danger personal to him. And lastly, part of him was also excited in a weird way; part of him wanted to leave this place behind, and all that it had come to represent, to get away, even for a little while.

Yesterday evening, when he had taken a much-needed shower, he had started to question the reality of his dreamscapes; and in extension of that, he was beginning to confront his apparent reliance on them. And there was a certain ambivalence to it; he was simultaneously looking forward to and dreading them, when falling asleep at night, and disappointed or relieved depending on whether or not he had experienced them, when waking up. As the last drops of water from the shower head splashed on the porcelain enamel of the bathtub, Jannus had a strange premonition that *if* he should follow through on this thing, then maybe he would get his answers. That *maybe* he would find his way out of this malaise. And either the whole thing would end, or he might find new beginnings. He hoped for the latter, yet expected the former.

And that night he dreamed.

CHAPTER VIII

The Kingdom of the Clouds

Jannus found himself above the clouds, walking under the clear, pristine sun. The whole thing seemed magical, yet the cloud-ground underneath him *felt* real enough. He was not walking *directly* on the clouds though; as far as he could see before him, there were paths of what looked to be soft crystal; a mirror-like surface that seemed to serve as walkways, almost like a sidewalk you would find in the world underneath the clouds.

The sun seemed unnaturally close, though Jannus knew very well that the sun would not look especially closer below or above the clouds; but maybe it was different here in the dreamscape. He was grateful that though the daystar seemed closer, he did not burn.

He spent a few moments just turning this way and that, not knowing where to go, and having no sense of direction here. There were only the clouds, the walkways, and the sun and the sky. And yet, as he looked again, the view before him had changed. He saw marble pillars, and golden arches. Crystal towers in the far distances, and in between it all, he saw gardens of vibrant green and violet. And with a blink of an eye, it disappeared from his vision again.

Jannus picked a direction at random. *South,* his instincts told him, though he had no way to verify that. In the beginning he walked alone, as he always did at the start of the dreamscape. Maybe it always took a while for Mielle to find him. And sure enough, he had only walked for a few hundred feet on the soft crystal surface (from what he could ascertain), before he saw a shadowy figure approach him in the distance. As she got closer, Jannus could see that Mielle looked more dishevelled than ever. Her amethyst robes were in absolute tatters, she had a scar on one cheek, and in her hands, she held her crown, now broken.

But she smiled at him, and he was reassured.

'Greetings, Jannus, how fares thee?' she said, as they stood before one another.

'Well enough, my lady,' he answered politely. He was somewhat disturbed by her visage, juxtaposed with her greeting, as if the two did not match exactly. 'Are you all right, Mielle?' Jannus asked her, curious.

Mielle gave him a puzzled look, not understanding, and in that very moment, her attire changed to their usual eminence. Mielle herself had not seemed to notice. Something held Jannus back from asking her further about her state, and after a few moments of awkward silence, they walked together, side by side, on what he thought was the southern path. Mielle seemed to be content with following whatever path he would take while here. Jannus had noticed that Mielle had seemed relatively quieter in this dreamscape. And out of the corner of his eyes, she seemed to flicker from time to time, as if she was losing substance. When he had asked her about this, Mielle had just shrugged her shoulders and smiled sadly.

'Time was never my most fearsome enemy, dear Jan,' she had told him. 'But forever might be.' *Cryptic as ever,* he had thought wryly, and refrained from further questioning, since that would undoubtedly lead to more mystery. Not only was Mielle quieter this time around, but also more distant in certain ways.

It took a while for Jannus to realise another oddity. Maybe as a consequence of their own silence, he noticed the *general* silence, in this particular dreamscape; before, he would always be able to hear the crashing waves, or the running river, the merciless wind, or even distant cries. But here, there was almost complete silence. Even their footsteps on the walkways were without sound. Only their breathing could be heard, and even that seemed much lighter than usual. In certain places along the pathways, the way forward was covered in mist, yet as they approached, it seemed to evaporate before them. The second time it happened, at an intersection, Jannus noticed that Mielle muttered under her breath.

In the distance, the huge shadow form of what had looked to be a mountain-top rising through the clouds, had now become clearer. Jannus could now see that it was in fact an iceberg, coloured bluish-white, that had penetrated the clouds. It had a somewhat strange shape to it, as it was halfway melted by the unbroken heat of the daystar. Part of it was melted in a way that gave it a shape like the tail of a whale. *What a strange association,* Jannus thought, as he and Mielle stood side by side about twenty feet from it.

Looking around, Jannus thought he could see other great shadows in the distance. Some shapes were too far away to see clearly, and so they remained shadows, at least from this vantage point. Other shapes were nearer; a few looked like other icebergs, not too different to the one right in front of the. Other shadows looked to be more defined, and almost square-shaped, with clearly outlined spire-shapes just above them. *Castles?* he thought. *Fortresses?* It suddenly dawned on him that there might very well be a whole world up here, beyond the clouds. Or maybe, there *used* to be a world, a civilisation, a kingdom even, up here, unseen and unwitnessed by most. Most of what he could see was covered in mist, which made it almost impossible to see what lay further beyond. From here, he could see only the shadows of all the gold and the crystal and the arches, as they flickered in and out of existence.

Initially, he was mesmerized by the amazing sights, yet as Jannus studied the ice itself on the iceberg right in front of them, he soon became horrified. Through the half-transparent surface, Jannus could see the shapes of human bodies, frozen in time. Fascinated and incredulous in equal measure, he stopped closer to the half-melted iceberg, and almost touched his chin to the ice. Mielle had refrained from stepping closer, and kept a respectable distance.

Jannus thought that he might hear a soft whisper; leaning closer, they spoke of ancient battles, won and lost. They spoke of courage and fear, and light and shadow; they spoke of men and mountains, both reaching for the sky. And lastly, they spoke of their fall and their end, their last stand. Or rather, they did not *speak* as such; it was more a story told in flashes and images that assaulted his mind.

'You should have seen us,' he heard them sigh. *'You should have seen us.'* And he almost could. Something prompted Jannus to touch the icy surface with his hand; it felt smooth and cool to the touch. He had expected it to be much colder, though, like touching a lamppost in winter with your fingertips or, even more foolishly, your tongue. This was more akin to water from the tap, at the coldest setting. For a few seconds nothing happened. But then, he was flooded with a series of images. *In his mind, he was transported to another place, a crystal cave of sorts, with stones the colour of red and green and black. And in between these, Jannus could see several pools of water. His vision in the cave was quite clear, though he could see no apparent source of illumination. He stepped closer to one of the pools; there were rings in the water, as if someone had just thrown in a stone. And as he kept looking, the ripples continued outward, though no one threw stones. At*

least, not anyone that Jannus could see. A sudden flash from the water emerged, white and violet, and almost blinded him. When he could see again, the image in the water was clear. He saw wild nature, unspoiled, and untouched and unbroken. He saw animals of every time that had ever been walking freely, unmindful of any threat.

The images shifted, and he saw how the wild nature had become more managed and controlled, he saw steel cages and iron chains. He saw retracted claws and dulled teeth.

A new image showed civilizations at their height and might, empires in all their glory and pride; with high towers of glass and savage weapons of war.

And lastly, Jannus witnessed an image of a wasteland, dry and empty, devoid of life and breath. He saw a place where no one walked any more. No one talked or cried or laughed. There was no sound but the wind passing by, and an old tired daystar above, starting to flicker...

With a start, Jannus removed his hand from the icy surface and took a few steps back, awed by the vision he had been granted.

'What happened here, Mielle?' Jannus croaked.

'I'm not sure, Jannus,' she answered, still behind his back. Jannus thought her voice sounded just a bit hesitant.

'It seemed like they fought a battle and lost,' Jannus said.

'That sounds like horrible dispraise, Jannus,' Mielle said, now sounding slightly concerned. He looked over his shoulder at her, but she kept her eyes fixed on the iceberg and the frozen bodies within.

'They fought their best here,' she continued. 'Here they still try to rest in peace, reaching for what they thought was right.'

Jannus thought that Mielle sounded almost as though she was edifying the frozen souls. Something about what she had said disturbed him.

'Try to?' he asked her. She had moved up beside them. She was holding her crown in a tender way, Jannus thought, as if almost caressing it, though she simultaneously acted as if unaware of its reappearance. 'Are they not at rest?'

'Nay.' She spoke softly, as if not wanting to disturb the trapped corpses. 'Only moribund, getting closer to release.'

Shocked, he took a few steps back, holding an arm out, defensively. Maybe he had not imagined their whispers then? It seemed like Mielle was reading his mind.

'Does this sting your conscience, Jan?' she asked him, almost teasingly. 'Imponderable, is it not?' she continued. A small smile was on her lips. Jannus noticed that her tattered robes were shifting a bit. The winds were rising, impossibly so. 'Aye, Jannus, these souls are not at rest. Not in any way imaginable.' She stopped close to the icy surface. Closest to her was a frozen figure, somewhat smaller than the rest. *A child, maybe,* Jannus, thought, in horror, as Mielle shifted her tone and told him another story.

A small girl looked up at her parents in confusion. She had tried all she could to figure out the puzzle they had lain on the ground before her feet. Nine different blocks in three different sizes and shapes that were supposed to make some sort of harmonic pattern, if chosen and placed in the correct manner. The girl had tried and tried, before — with a heavy heart — she looked up at her parents, dreading their response to her failure. And yet they only smiled at her, prompting her to continue her efforts. And so she tried, and tried again, and yet she obtained no harmony, and any semblance of correctness seemed to elude her. The girl looked up at her parents again; their smiles remained, but only with their mouths. Their eyes had lost their warmth for their ailing daughter, and she felt them retreating. Not physically, but emotionally, and so she tried ever harder to please them. And the harder she tried, and failed, the faster her mother and father moved away.

It took a while for Jannus to realise that Mielle had stopped telling her tale; her story had once again caught his attention in more ways than once. He empathised with the girl as he recognised himself in relation to his own parents. But he had also met a lot of children like that girl in the story, all former clients who had, in one way or another, felt as if they had failed someone in their life. Jannus became aware that his pulse was racing.

Once again, she was cognisant of his anxiousness. 'No cause for alarm, dear Jannus', she said, her voice full of compassion. 'The winds are but an intermittent occurrence here. That is not what should worry you.' She stepped closer, and he looked into her eyes, so filled with ancient remorse.

'The winds are but passing you by; the object of your worry remains solely in your heart.' Suddenly, Jannus sensed something change. Something had shifted in his immediate surroundings, as if the *rules* had been changed. And he felt himself *falling.* Through the clouds and down and down and down.

'With blind covetousness and foolish anger,' Mielle recited in her observations. The sky had been calm, so very calm that she almost saw it as an aberration. 'With injurious shade they came when all amity was lost, as we hurt and we fled,' she continued. She wished everything well for the man Jannus, even though she she had not been entirely truthful; how she had never told him of her own truth at all, and yet how she had almost revealed too much. How she, once upon a time, had forgotten all jurisprudence for the sake of ideals of her own making. And how she had savoured that single apple-bite, and had wanted to claim the rest of it. 'One soul, and one heart, free of his chains, and maybe I shall be free of mine,' she whispered, and the rising wind took her words far way.

CHAPTER IX

Sleep, Old Friend

Jannus awoke the next morning, predictably unrested, feeling overwhelmed by last night's visions. He had been so overwhelmed, in fact, that he had succumbed to his vices. He knew it was a bad idea, like it had been so many times before. Jannus had opened his stash of liquid gold, just for a few snifters; just a little to get going... All the well-rehearsed lies and excuses.

Jannus had tried to resist; he had opened the closet, and closed it again. And then repeated the ritual several times over. It was an old corner-cabinet he had bought from a second-hand store, years ago. It had a key he usually kept beneath layers of socks in a drawer in the bedroom. That way, he had to go through several steps, which ideally should have provided more than one opportunity to stop himself.

Usually, it was enough. Most of the time, even. This time it had worked halfway; he had closed the cabinet a fourth time, locked it, and had even put the key back where it belonged. Along the way though, he had managed to take half of tomorrow's medicine. 'Zero chance of ever turning this around,' he had murmured, as he had finally poured himself an ounce or two. *It was always in there, sleeping. Almost like a friend you thought lost. Then, a short while after the re-emergence of your long-lost friend, you felt relief. But after a while, you wished your friend would have stayed away.*

By now, the day had passed lunchtime; outside seemed grey and dull. Dazed and confused by the drinks and the pills, Jannus had pulled out his backpack from the hallway closet. Still wrapped in plastic, he had never used it. In this most curious state, Jannus had decided to leave the house. He had searched the address in the letters, and now knew where it was. It was about seventy miles north-west of his present location. No surprise there: he had never moved too far from home. It would be only a short trip on a bus, or by car. Yet Jannus had decided that he would walk the journey; along the roads, or go cross-country. A small, almost forgotten part of his conscience realised that the walk might even be good for him.

During his search for the unused backpack, he found an old cardboard-box; a moving box in actuality. It was open, as if someone had just searched through it. Inside, there was a collection of old childhood memories. Among these, Jannus had found a cardboard cut-out of a yellow sun, on a green background, with six sunbeams of different colours, as if he had wanted to make some sort of artistically opalescent remark. It had been a gift from himself, to his grandmother. Thinking back through the grey haze of medicine and alcohol,

Jannus thought that he must have been about seven or eight years old at the time. He had never been very proficient in this type of work; you could still see the pencil markings, on which he was supposed to have used the scissors.

His grandmother had seemed grateful, though. She had smiled her gentle smile, and the next time Jannus came to visit, his cardboard cut-out had found its place hanging in her kitchen window. 'From there it will forever brighten and elucidate my every morning, sweet Jan,' he remembered her saying.

He had forgotten that yellow sun, and the gift he had made of it. In a sad association, he recalled how the light of the sun had turned to amber, as she lay dying. The backpack was almost full; clothes for a few days on the road, a printed-out map of the countryside, and a single bottle of dark liquor in reserve, just in case. He decided against taking his phone with him. He wanted to be free of any obligations, and it was only supposed to be a couple of days' worth of travel, anyway, at a slow pace. Travelling by the main roads would be a lot faster, but he had an urge to travel cross-country. Contrarily, he did leave a note on the kitchen counter, with a short message saying where he had gone to, and put some money in his pocket. Again, *just in case.*

For a while now, Jannus had in reality known about the origin of the address in the letter. Though he had tried to bury those memories in the abyss where they — in his regard — belonged, part of him had always known. It was an address in his hometown; just about forty-five miles north-west of here; just off the north-western edge of the peninsula. He had lived there for the first nineteen years of his life. Most of them had been miserable, and he had got out of there just as soon as he had completed his secondary education. After that, he had tried never to look back, except in absolute emergencies. Though he had never moved more than fifty miles away from his homestead, he had tried to forget. It was not his exact childhood-home address; it was the name of his father's workplace, a place that he had never been inside, but had represented only something unknown, and unapproachable. It was a place he had never ventured to as a child, and never gone back to as an adult. Not physically, at least. Mentally, it had stood as an oppressing force he had tried to escape for many years, and mostly tried to avoid ever since. Yet no matter how he tried, something always remained with him, deep inside, buried deep, sleeping and dreaming. Until now.

His home town was not very big though; about four thousand people lived there, when he was growing up. He suspected that the number was even lower now; like so many of the smaller settlements on the peninsula, the population in his home had probably dwindled, and had joined the chorus of ghost-towns that were now so prevalent. Young people and families moved away to the bigger cities, for the perceived notion of safety in numbers, and greater job opportunities.

Jannus had moved away for safety reasons, too, albeit of a slightly different nature. His childhood home had been a cage, and moving away had meant freedom; a freedom that he prized above almost anything else. Mostly that had been beneficial, though also sometimes to his detriment, and also to his close relationships.

And so, even though part of him had recognised the address, Jannus had tried to avoid the reality of it; the reality of where his life began, and where he came from. So far, he had even made a decent job of it; in almost every attempt of engagement and confrontation throughout his life, since he left, he had met with avoidance in some manner. Ironically, this was a strategy often employed by quite a few of his former clients. Jannus had often consoled himself by the reminder that you had to learn from the best; and he was very well equipped to teach people how not to avoid the difficult things in life, though he had plenty of experience of not actually abiding by the same standards.

What prompted him to return this time was still unclear to him, though. Curiosity? Desperation? Jannus was unsure. Maybe it was because he had nothing better to do? Or that he did not have much to lose any more? *Or drunk and medicated?* he mused.

As he closed the backpack, and put one strap over his right shoulder, he had a moment of hesitation in the hallway. With one hand closed around the front-door handle, he looked one final time over his shoulder.

There was not much to return to, even if he would. In truth, this place had just been another somewhere for him to hide, at least these past few years. Gathering what courage remained in him, he opened the door, stumbled on the threshold, and ventured out into the wilds.

And the gentleman of leisure knew that things were fast approaching, the moment was almost imminent, the wait was almost over. He had kept waiting and waiting and waiting for so long for the shadows to evaporate, for the veil to clear. And now, the moment was at hand. The confrontation was finally here, the moment of absolute breaking almost within his reach. Just a few moments more, my dear, then all would become clear. He had very nearly been undone by his patience, yet now his reward was close to being harvested; the time of a man's reckoning was here.

PART II

ON ROADS LESS TRAVELLED

CHAPTER X

I Should Have Come Over

It was no ordinary love that they had shared, Jannus and his former wife. Like all couples, they had had good times and bad times; yet what had brought them together back then was still a mystery to him, as was whatever had held them together for as long as they were. Such thoughts filled his mind as he was seeking shelter from the rain under an abandoned tin-roofed half-shed. The shed was missing its door, so Jannus was not completely safe from the downpour that had suddenly erupted from the sky. He had left the last town behind early this morning; the place had been covered in mist, yet the skies had cleared during the first few hours of walking. Jannus had admired the fields of green and gold beginning just outside the town borders. Walking along the high road coursing its way in between the fields, he first stumbled upon a collection of ramshackle houses. Jannus knew this indicated that the town used to encompass a broader place in the northwestern direction. The half-torn-down houses were another reminder that quite a few people had moved away from these districts to find better opportunities.

Gazing inside some of the houses through broken walls, Jannus could see that some people had even left some of their belongings behind; a child had even left a teddy bear in the dirt, forever deemed unworthy of a possible new future. Jannus had noted that the bear had looked worn and ragged, and had even lost one of its button-eyes. He had seen a lot more unworthy things left behind, yet the sight of the one-eyed bear was the one that remained with him.

Just short of an hour beyond the houses, the skies had darkened again, and the downpour began. Jannus had found no immediate shelter on the high road, seeing mostly green and gold. And so, he walked beneath the rains, getting fairly drenched, until he came upon this half-shed. He did not know what had prompted his reflections of his former wife; he thought he had left her far behind. Or rather, that *she* was the one that had left *him* behind, if he was to be completely honest with himself. In a way, he was the broken-down house or maybe the one-eyed teddy-bear left behind in the dirt, while she had travelled the high road in between the fields of green and gold, mist covering the land behind her, forgotten in time and space.

The first few years of their life together had been almost without argument or incident. At least, that was how Jannus remembered it; or maybe that was just the old pertinacity showing its influence again. He poked his head out of the shed, to get a feel for the strength of the downpour; it seemed to be lessening somewhat. If he was lucky, it would pass within the hour, and he could continue on his way.

There was not any chair in the half-shed, but it did contain an old wooden box that Jannus (after a short inspection) chose to utilise as a seat. It was somewhat wobbly, so he decided not to put his full weight on it. The poor condition of the wooden box and the half-shed as a whole somehow reminded Jannus of his father's office, in their mansion home, though that place had seemed like this one's diametrical opposite. The office, ordained with wood panels, carved, and enamelled, had always been a 'keep-out' area, with regard to Jannus, at least. There was not to be a mark or blemish of any kind, little boy Jannus had been made painfully aware, more than once. Given a choice, he would prefer the wobbly and weather-beaten wooden box now presently beneath him, to that room of apparent perfection.

Jannus pulled on the sleeves of his jacket; out of all the things he had packed for the trip, somehow, he had neglected a rain coat. The weather had seemed clear enough when he set out, yet he was well-aware of its random nature in these parts, having lived here for most of his adult life.

The weather. That was just such a thing that he and his former wife could begin to argue about. Something trivial, something unimportant. Jannus could not, for the life of him, begin to understand why it had such importance and relevance to his former wife. It could be about anything, really. From the weather to something in the news. From footwear to orange juice, and even classic nuisances such as milk-cartons and open toilet-seats got their screen-time. The latter two he could understand, even though he sometimes had to plead forgetfulness quite a few times in those instances. But not the other ones. As a therapist, he had never ventured into couple's counselling; Jannus had always found it stressful, even more than group-therapy, which did not make immediate sense. Yet, a few years after he had waved goodbye to that particular branch of life, the former therapist had finally realised what had been the issue; it was too close to home, too near what was really going on in his own life. Not that you couldn't deal with therapeutic issues that you had issues with yourself, at one time or another, but it usually entailed some level of transparency about it, and quite a bit of distance to it, as well. Otherwise, you could find yourself too mired in your own misery to be able to objectively assist the individual in the chair just across from you.

'Why do you do that?' Jannus had once asked his former wife.

She had not looked up from her endeavour, apparently ignoring him to his growing dissatisfaction. They sat together at the kitchen table as they had so many times before, eating breakfast together in the early morning. It had been a cold morning, inside and outside. His own preferred breakfast consisted of a simple piece of toast with cheese, and two charred slices of tomato on top, and to wash it down, a glass of milk and a mug of coffee. His wife's breakfast routines changed regularly, making the term 'regular' ill-fitting. With one exception; she had a piece a toast on her plate, just like Jannus. On top, she had two layers of marmalade, each carefully spread on the piece of toast with a teaspoon. The bottom layer was strawberry, the top one boysenberry.

She had never explained to him this ritual, though Jannus had tried to ask several times. Each time she had deflected, sometimes in silence, other times short and sharp, and even a few times with a violent outburst. The last time it had looked to be a treatment of silence.

He had been down to his last few bites of toast, cheese and tomato, when she had finally looked at him. Just a few seconds before, Jannus been irritated at her for seemingly ignoring him; now he wished she had kept at her ritual, rather than looking at him.

'Why is it that important for you to know, Jan?' she had asked him. Not angrily, but tired. *So* tired, he recalled.

'I just want to know,' he had said, stupidly. He took a last sip of milk, and held his mug with the remaining morning coffee in it. He had held it to his mouth without actually drinking it, waiting for her answer. He had made the foolish assumption that she would actually provide him with an answer this time.

'That's not enough, Jannus,' she had finally said, taking a few tiny bites of the toast. That was another thing that had irritated him no end; she took forever to eat her food, while Jannus himself gulped down his own, as if afraid someone would come and take it away from him.

'Why?' he had somehow managed to insist. He had felt angry and frustrated, yet something had made him wonder as well; she had not raised her voice so far. The timbre in her voice had not betrayed any hint of anger on her part. She had just seemed tired, and apathetic, still following her routines, but not an inch more than that. That realisation had made him feel worthless, and petrified, as if there was nothing more he could do.

She had put down her toast, and taken a few sips of her morning tea (herbal, by the scent; as ever, it changed as per her whim), before she had given him a final answer.

'It's an old thing, Jannus… from… before.' Jannus had been holding his breath in equal parts of optimistic anticipation and dread. 'Before you, I mean.' She had smiled at him, a smile so sad and tired that he had wanted to scream. On some level it had reminded him of something, that smile. And whenever he thought back to that morning, with each of them eating their piece of toast, that smile had signified the beginning of the end. Jannus still wondered, at times, what would have happened if he had not sat there, petrified, while she finished her meal, and left for work. What if he had said something, *anything?* What if he had reached out a hand in comfort? Or gone to her side in a warm embrace? Maybe the end would have been different? Or maybe there would not even have *been* an end?

Back to the present and never short of misgivings, Jannus looked out from his shelter. It looked as though the rain had begun to dissipate. As he walked on towards his destination, a few more flashes of memory of their relationship resurfaced; some warmed him on his path, others left him as cold as the end had turned out to be.

A flash of yellow; the summer sun burned above them. Their garden was green and brown and yellow and purple, with a single red slash from a red tulip that had somehow found its way between the yellow and purple; his wife's absolute favourites. She was working hard with her hands in the dirt; he was reclining, and enjoying his day. The only thing interrupting his peace was her exasperation. He did not mind, though; not at this point. As each of her grunts from her garden-work became louder and louder, his smile somehow became wider and wider. At this point, Jannus had opened one eye in anticipation of what he knew would come next; soon, she would begin cursing, first to herself, and the progressing to the extent whereby the neighbours would hear. Before that had happened, he had burst out laughing, not able to contain himself. She had jerked her head back at him, sweat on her brow from exertion. 'Would you mind giving me a hand here, Jan?' she had asked him in mock anger.

'Of course, my dear,' he had answered her, without the slightest hint of bitterness.

A flash of deep purple: Jannus *sat on the couch in the living room. His wife was in the bedroom, cleaning up. After him. He had been up late last night; it was not a case of him returning home from some night out — oh no. He had spent the whole evening the day before, and even most of the night, right here on this very couch. He could not recall, but he thought his wife might have talked to him during the evening, maybe even shouted at him. About what he could not say. Maybe something about turning the volume down on the television? Or maybe turning it off completely. Yesterday was a haze. He must have stumbled into bed in the early morning. Half an hour ago, just before midday, he had returned to the living, albeit with half his face covered in his own vomit. His wife had shouted something unintelligible at him; the specifics had escaped him, as they had been doing for a while. Now, with face washed clean of vomit,* Jannus *had resumed his place in the living room couch, the precious liquid gold in glass containers in front of him, ready to be devoured, as he himself would drown.*

Oh, how your rain of tears forms rivers in the dark, Jannus; *is your misery written in blood? Is it your own sacrifice, or did you choose the coward's way, as always? The gentleman of leisure thought his dark thoughts, buried deep within. Finally, he had stood up, and walked away from the rickety chair in the middle of the room. He had spent the last hour or so walking around it on the dusty, creaky floorboards, dragging his chains behind him. Usually, he would have no notion of the time in this abandoned building, yet someone seemed to have left one of the blinds half-open; the cursed light of the sun kept creeping across the floor. When he walked by the chair closest to the windows, the gentleman instinctively shied away from the sunlight, whenever it would hit his pale feet.*

'At your heart, the frozen lake of treachery,' he recited from somewhere. From where exactly, he could not say. Maybe from one of those picaresque stories he had so loved in his young adult days, a time now misremembered, if not forgotten altogether. The only remnant from that time was the promise to himself that he would never succumb to human indifference, that he would never break the oath that he would lose his grip of his youthful exuberance. And most of all, that he would remain sanguine. As he was dragging his chains behind him, sunlit floorboards creaking, the gentleman of leisure knew that he had lost all three long ago. Only the upcoming confrontation kept him going, around and around the rickety chair.

CHAPTER XI

The Ways of Silver

Jannus decided to rest his feet, chancing upon a small creek not far from the high road. Traffic had tightened, and he had been annoyed by the cacophony, turning west until all the sounds were but a distant murmur. He began to recognise the scenery somewhat; Jannus could not see it from this distance, but he knew that if he continued in this direction, he would be able to see the great forest, a well-known landscape from his childhood days.

Kneeling down by the stream, Jannus felt comforted by the gentle sounds of the water. Above, the daystar had broken through the clouds again, which made the surface glimmer, crystal-like. It reminded him of another image from one of his dreamscapes; the water curtains of the tail of some great whale unfurling, silver-crystals shimmering like thousands of fireflies. This, in turn, had reminded him of yet another vision: that of the icebergs spearing through the clouds in that lost, forgotten kingdom.

Walking cross-country, walking through harmonic green and blissful gold, he was somehow reminded of another event from his past — this time, from 'real life'. Not too long ago, Jannus had made yet another visit to his doctor, just for a general examination; the ones they provided to certain people of certain ages and conditions. The test results were decent enough, but Jannus recalled that his doctor's features had been marred by a curious frown.

'So, Mr Rubens,' the doctor had announced. 'Everything looks... reasonable, I suppose you could say.' Jannus had felt anger at the doctor's words, exposing him just like that! 'You're somewhat out of shape, as you probably know.' The doctor had looked up from the journal, held eye-contact for just a while, and had given Jannus one of his short, sharp smiles, with just a thin line of teeth showing. 'Like a killer shark,' his former wife would have so eloquently formulated with her own, much grander, showing of teeth.

'I recommend a change of diet, and exercise, Mr Rubens.' He had given Jannus another look, and then pointed a most unprofessional finger at him. 'As I told you before, *Jan,* this cannot go on much longer.' Then he had slammed the journal on the table, and had stood up from his seat. Standing, he had towered over Jannus, who was already feeling insignificant enough. 'If you go on like this, Mr Rubens, you're looking at an early grave.' When Jannus had made (yet) another promise that he would follow the doctor's advice, and was heading out the door, his doctor had made one final announcement. 'Do not follow in your father's footsteps, Jannus. You have done a job good not doing so until now. It would be a shame to see you misstep at this point. Truly.' Jannus had not turned around at those words, yet those words had stuck with him. At the time, he had been so flabbergasted that he had forgotten to ask his doctor about how he even *knew* about his father.

And now, trudging through the field, he was reminded of his doctor's words. Jannus was walking only at a steady, tempered pace, but his pulse was almost galloping, and the sounds of his heavy breathing resounded in his head. When he had heard and found the stream, Jannus had felt relief at the excuse for a short rest.

Kneeling down by the running waters, Jannus realised that his doctor was, unfortunately, right. He had never been athletic, by any means, but he seemed to recall that he had been a pretty fair runner; not the best in class, to be sure, but above the average. And his general activity level had been much higher, just until a few years ago. It had not been an abrupt drop, but a somewhat steady decline. Jannus let one hand drift this way and that in the summer-cool stream. He looked up. Beyond the stream was a great field of brown earth with golden patches here and there. And beyond that, the great forest. He knew he could follow the high road and go the long way around to his hometown. Or, he could go through the forest, which *could* potentially be a slow path as well, unless you knew it as well as Jannus did.

As a child he had often gone there; it had been a

sort of refuge, a place of shadow and mystery, and adventure. Looking at it from this distance, he wondered what it would feel like as an adult. Would it retain its sense of wonder? Would he still feel the slightest tinge of fear at the slightest sounds from some unseen entity in the shadows? Would his childish imagination take him away this time around? Would he be easily led astray through the unknown paths of wood and leaf and shadow as he had been back then? Or would his adult-self remain in command and reject all possibility of charm and wonder?

Jannus felt something touch his hand in the water; he supposed it could have been a passing fish, but because of the shimmering surface, he could not be certain. As he was looking around, he noticed some of the greenery growing near the stream. He recognised a few of them: he saw northern fir moss and blue heath; he noticed red rattle and even spotted a single arctic alprose. His grandmother had been quite the naturalist, and had kept a few books with pictures and descriptions of a lot of plants and flowers. Jannus could even recall some of it. He looked again at the singular rose; he could not remember if any of these plants were meant to grow by the edge of the water, or even if they were meant to grow near one another. Somehow, he thought not. The silver surface of the water played tricks on his eyes, the sun went in hiding behind a cloud, and the day darkened just a bit.

These last few days had been a blur, Jannus

reflected; the dreamscapes used to appear only at night, only in sleep. Now, they seemed to surface whenever; in short moments of reflection, even while doing a chore, Jannus would now suddenly get an image of something, or the voice of someone just nearby, yet unseen. The former therapist was growing increasingly worried that something was wrong with him.

Jannus decided that this place might be well suited for a resting spot, or makeshift campsite of sorts. The day had become greyer, and he judged the time to be late afternoon, or maybe early evening. He removed the backpack, and felt an ache in his lower back, as he twisted around. As Jannus massaged his back, he looked around him, curiously. The grass along the creek seemed greener and brighter than the field he had been walking through, probably because of the proximity of the water. It would also provide him with a somewhat comfortable place to sit or lay down.

Jannus heard and felt his stomach rumble; apparently it was not only his back that craved attention after his labours. He opened his backpack and took out a few of his supplies; two pieces of bread with butter and cheese, together with one of the oranges he had bought the other day. Suddenly, Jannus frowned, as he looked through the rest of the backpack. Not finding what he was looking for, he started to panic.

'Where is it? Where *is* it?!' Jannus asked aloud, as if expecting someone to retort. Only the stream beside him gave a bubbling answer, which was not satisfactory at all. Irritated at himself, he emptied the whole backpack, even turning it upside down to make sure. And sure enough, he had forgotten to pack his medicines, his daily supplements of balance and calm. *And my synthesised crutches,* he thought, feeling both angry and anxious.

It took Jannus several minutes to calm down again; he focused on his breathing, and the sounds of the water beside him, ever bubbling, and blissfully unaware. As he refilled his backpack, he grabbed hold of the bottle he had brought with him, just in case. It lured with its copper-gold content, almost playing tricks with his eyes as the surface of the water in the stream. Jannus turned this bottle this way and that in his hands, silently debating with himself, trying to make a choice.

In the end he decided against it; he still had a while to go, maybe a day or two, and he might need it along the way. *More so than now, maybe,* he thought, as his anxiety slowly receded, yet did not disappear completely. Janus completed repacking, found a good spot for the backpack in the grass, sat down, and rested his back against it.

With bread and orange and water in hand, Jannus looked up the darkened sky; the daystar was almost not visible as it settled. He would continue onward tomorrow, following his current north-west direction. Until then he would try to get some rest, as best he could.

Maybe it was his own anxiety, or maybe his anger,

that made the former therapist think of one of his very first clients, back when he had just earned his degree. He had been so excited back then, and just a tad naïve, maybe. 'I'm a prisoner not yet given a number, Doc,' his client had pronounced when he had seen Jannus for the first time. This particular client had been part of a resocialisation-programme. As a requirement of his early release, he had to attend a psychologist (and a psychiatrist). Jannus' first job had been at the Prison Service, where part of the work was writing evaluations, and performing therapeutic sessions with the inmates. Somehow it had been decided that Jannus should be the one to talk to this particular client. And Jannus had not had the necessary experience to know his professional limits, at the time.

And he had liked this client well enough. In the beginning, anyway. He had been sympathetic at first glance. Maybe that had been a particular gift of his. The client had told Jannus of his early-life experiences, and how, step by step, he had found himself developing a criminal lifestyle, finding it more and more difficult to choose another path. 'Money changed hands, starting slow with silver coins, then gold, and finally with stacks of cotton and linen, Doc.' The client had kept calling Jannus a 'Doc', though that was technically not true. 'I fell on darkened days, Doc, I sure did,' he had told the young therapist with an empathetic smile, and eyes full of false sorrow.

Every session would be interrupted by a knock on

the door to the almost empty room in which Jannus had sat with his Prison Service clients, followed by the sound of heavy key chains. Then the guard for the day would open the door, and take the clients, now turned prisoners, back to their designated rooms again. Jannus would remain in the room for just a while longer, either to wait for the next one in line, or to gather his thoughts, and write his notes.

'That's the jailer, Doc, coming to take me home,' this most singular client would remark with a smile, as his hands had been chained in grey and silver. Jannus would never find out whatever happened to him on his release; he only knew he had been on the run from some of the criminal groups he had been associated with before the authorities got to him. 'Lucky me, eh, Doc?' the client had told Jannus.

Why Jannus would think of this particular client at this specific moment was beyond his comprehension. He realised that these were important days for him; he could either continue on the way he had been these last few years, and most likely reach his end before long, just like his pater, or he could try to make a change, however futile it might seem.

Looking back, Jannus knew that in the therapy room he could have been described as obsequious; outside that room, not so much. Outside, he was much more disengaged, almost disinterested and aloof. Not much got through to him, in truth, as if every ray of light from the daystar had to go through a too-small aperture, not big enough to properly illuminate whatever needed the light. Jannus knew he had difficulty making concessions, especially in close relations. And every concession he *did* make had hurt, the memory of it forever ingrained with deep-sinking hooks.

Looking back on his life so far, his failures seemed to stand out the most somehow, as if they had blocked his view over time, making everything distorted and dreary. Jannus' impression was that he was looking through a lens of despair, never able to see the sweetest thing right in front of him, silver-wings getting too small for flight. *To remember forever is part of my doom, having forsaken the shores of Lethe.* The old poetic lines resurfaced in his mind as he looked on the singular alprose gently swaying in the wind, which had begun to pick up somewhat, while he knelt at the stream's edge. He frowned. None of the plants he had noticed seemed to move; they were completely still, as if frozen or held in abeyance.

He had never considered himself *sui generis*, or anything special, despite keeping himself isolated and apart. It was not that he *wanted* to feel like someone special, or something significant. It had more to do with the fact that he wanted to feel *a part* of something. And not so alone.

As he lay on the soft ground, leaning against his backpack, Jannus suddenly felt a chill on his neck, though he had not noticed any significant change in temperature. He got the sensation that something had lightly brushed his shoulder; it felt somewhat like the touch of a delicate hand, or maybe a piece of soft cloth pressed against the skin. He turned around, but saw nothing. And then a barely heard whisper beneath the wind; *Follow your star to a haven most glorious, Jan.* Startled, Jannus turned around again, and continued to see nothing. To the soothing sounds of the stream beside him, he eventually fell asleep; this time, mercifully, without dreams of any kind.

CHAPTER XII

Johan of the Outer Isles

Getting closer, Jannus could see that the man looked to be a vagabond of sorts; he wore a leather vest with a lot of emblems of every variety on it. On his head, the man had a leather cap, likewise ornamented with all manner of flair. It did not look like the stranger had a lot of hair on his head (except maybe hidden under the cap), but instead, he sported a great white beard, or maybe platinum blond; it was difficult to tell. At his side, was a baby-carriage, worn with age, filled up with all manner of plastic and paper bags. The vagabond was sitting on a fold-out chair and was looking down, hands folded over an ample belly, as if asleep, or maybe contemplating.

Jannus had been walking for several hours, trudging through what felt like swampy fields and uncultivated ground. It had been raining a lot, and the sky was still a dark grey, threatening to erupt once again.

He had seen the man from quite a distance; after all, there was not much else to see on this swampy field of brown and gold. The man seemed heavy-set, and sat down next to some colourful contraption. While walking, Jannus considered changing direction to avoid meeting the man. But then he thought it a silly notion, and trudged on towards his destination. He would give a polite nod to the man, and carry on. He had to be mindful of his steps here; it was slow going indeed.

As he prepared to walk past the stranger, the man suddenly gave a start, and looked up. Sighing, Jannus picked up his step, trying to avoid attention. It proved too late.

'Why, hey there, good fellow,' the vagabond greeted him. Cursing silently, Jannus turned to the man, hoping to end the interaction as quickly as possible. The stranger had found a small patch of ground with relatively firm footing.

'Well enough,' he managed. 'I'm just on my way to somewhere important, so if you'll excuse—'

The vagabond had started nodding as soon as Jannus began talking. 'Places to be, people to see, eh?' he said, and looked at Jannus with a knowing grin on his face.

The vagabond took out two beers from one of the bags in the carriage, offered one of them to Jannus (who declined), opened the other one with a smart motion, and took a great, big gulp. When he was done, he looked again at Jannus, this time with a satisfied smile under the beard. *White, with silver strains,* Jannus thought, absently.

'I knew right away what kind of man you were. Oh yes I did,' the vagabond said, pointing the can at him. 'A busy man, I said to myself, a busy man indeed. I've seen them before!' The man took another drink of his beer, this time a modest sip. 'I've been one myself. Once, sure enough!'

Despite himself, Jannus grew curious. 'How so?' he asked the vagabond.

'Do you want to know?' the man asked him. 'Truly? Are you certain you have the time?' The vagabond's gaze was somehow penetrating, and his knowing grin was becoming infuriating to Jannus. Looking up, the daystar had not yet made a reappearance, and the skies remained a dark grey.

'Seeking shelter from the storm, eh?' the vagabond asked, again shrewdly. Jannus was about to voice his disagreement, then changed his mind, and shook his head. The stranger simply nodded, apparently understanding. Jannus saw a small, single, brass plate on the man's vest on the right side of his chest. Written on the plate he could read the words: "Cutting Grinder." The meaning of it escaped Jannus.

Having finished his beer, the vagabond threw it in one of the half-open plastic bags in the carriage; by the sound of it, the empty can was joining quite a few of its peers. The vagabond's breathing was heavy and ragged, and he looked to be gathering his strength. Jannus wondered if the simple act of finishing his beer and throwing it aside was enough to tire the stranger. There were a couple of seconds of silence, the only sound being the vagabond's laboured breath. Slowly, he told his tale to Jannus, who, for some unknown reason, chose to stay to listen, this one time. The vagabond did not look to encompass any sort of sartorial elegance, by any means, yet Jannus (surprised at himself) found that he somehow took a liking to the man, almost immediately; well, after his initial mandatory trepidation of any kind of human encounter, anyway.

'I left my home twenty-five years ago,' the vagabond began. He was still smiling, yet this time it was not the self-assured sort of spectacle that Jannus had first witnessed. 'I had a wife and everything, you know!' The vagabond laughed softly, then coughed a few times. *Maybe he's used to laughing,* Jannus thought. *Or talk.*

'Everything was set and done. I was ready to go.' The man leaned forward, then almost lost his balance, the fold-out chair probably lacking in constitution with the man's weight currently placed upon it. Jannus stepped forward quickly, but the vagabond was even faster in regaining his balance. Maybe he was experienced in this; the fold-out chair looked pretty worn, yellow paint flaking here and there, from what Jannus could see.

'That was a close one!' the stranger exclaimed, before he continued his tale. 'Aye, a wife and everything. A great woman, you know. And I was going to university, can you believe it?' The vagabond did not wait for Jannus to answer. 'Oh yes, Economics it was. Had a head for numbers back then. Still do, I suppose.' The man rearranged some of the emblems on his leather vest. Jannus got the clear impression that the vagabond was an experienced story-teller, and all-too willing to tell Jannus his tale.

'It was just too much, you know?' He looked at Jannus with wet eyes. Jannus thought the vagabond's lips trembled a bit, but the platinum-blond beard made a decent job of covering it up, if so. 'I found this old discarded pram you see here.' The stranger padded the stroller handle with a big and scarred hand. Jannus was strangely moved by that gesture.

'It was almost new, yet someone had thrown it out, anyway.' The old man shook his head in disgust. 'All new it was. Almost never used, it looked like.' Jannus thought the old man's smile looked sad and wistful, as if remembering lost days.

'I filled her up with what clothes I had, and an assortment of victuals and mayhap a bit of drink, and off I went!'

'Where did you go?' Jannus asked, now genuinely curious. He felt his legs starting to ache, and wanted to find a place to sit. But the only seat in sight — other than the ground — was the vagabond's fold-out chair, and Jannus had not lost that much decency to ask the old man for his seat. And so, he suffered in silence, and shook his legs, one after the other, while the stranger continued his tale.

'To my freedom, my boy, to my freedom.' The vagabond's white smile had returned in full force (though his eyes were still wet), and Jannus found himself returning the smile. 'Away from all the automatic and the monotony, away from the storm.' Jannus wanted to ask whatever the vagabond meant by 'storm', but chose not to comment. Instinctively, he thought he already knew.

Suddenly, flashes came upon his mind; he was not dreaming, but wide-awake, yet they came anyway: visions of a great block of broken-off ice looking like a floating turtle in the violent waters; red and silver-black rocks with white stripes lying dormant in their cold comfort, iridescences futilely in battle with the surrounding shadows.

'Are you okay, son?' Jannus felt the old man's hand on his shoulder; scarred, yet somehow soft to the touch. The former therapist found himself lying on the ground. Luckily, he had not hit anything as he went down; they were in the middle of a field, but even so he could have hit a half-hidden rock. The vagabond had risen from his chair, not quick enough to catch Jannus, but faster than Jannus might have expected, judging by the man's girth.

'I'm fine,' Jannus said, rising slowly to his feet. 'Just tired, that's all. Been walking for a while now.'

The vagabond nodded, as if understanding. 'To where?' he asked, regaining his seat.

Jannus dusted off his jeans from his fall before answering. 'I don't know, actually.' He suddenly remembered that he had started off the conversation with telling the old man that he was going somewhere *important.* Hoping to divert the stranger, he quickly found something to ask him. 'What is your name, by the way?' he blurted.

The vagabond looked behind Jannus, to the high road, perhaps. The sound of increasing traffic was distant, yet loud enough to hear. 'Johan of the Outer Isles,' I am called,' the old man said gently, so low that Jannus almost did not hear. 'Why, they call me that, and who began it, I do not know, son.' The vagabond, or *Johan,* looked back at Jannus. A single tear was running down one cheek until it was lost in the platinum-blond beard. Johan did not seem to have noticed. 'Well, the *first part* is true enough, I suppose.' Johan was getting another can from the carriage, maybe the one he had first offered Jannus.

'Twenty-five years ago, more or less. Married to a great woman back then, on my way to great things, as I said. On the expected path, ready to go.' Johan shook his head. 'Not for me, son, not for me.' Jannus noticed that the vagabond had yet to open the new can; maybe the old man was too absorbed in his own memories.

'Understand me, son, it was not a great moment of afflatus, or anything. I was given no sign, and no warning.' Johan looked to the carriage at his side, which Jannus now realised must have been his travelling companion all these years, since he had left his former life behind. The vagabond chuckled, and Jannus smiled at him, uncertain of the humour.

'There was no wrong done to me, son, you must understand. People wanted the best for me, I'm sure. My parents, they tried the best they could. And my wife...' Johan trailed off. Jannus was uncertain if he wanted to break the silence, or let the old man continue at his own pace.

'Do you hate her?' Jannus finally asked him, not knowing exactly why he wanted the answer to *that*.

Johan of the Outer Isles looked up in surprise. 'Hate? No, son. Not hate. Not ever. Not that.' Jannus found the vagabond's gaze piercing, and he kept quiet again. 'No contempt here, boy. Only *grief.*' Johan had still not opened the second can of beer, and the two men sat (well, one *stood)* in silence on the brown and golden field. The high road was still reminding them of its presence behind them, where the earth gave way to the tarmac, the cars and the trucks passing them by, unnoticed and unmindful of all.

'Well, now I make my way as a "knight of the road", as some people call us,' Johan guffawed, and Jannus found himself laughing with the old man. 'You wouldn't know it looking at me, son, but I still have some important duties of my own among these peers of mine on these roads.' Putting back the second can of beer, he counted off the fingers on his left hand with his right. 'I'm quite good at solving disputes, where they may arise; I'm fairly good with words, and sometimes people gather to hear me speak my tales; and I like to give a helping hand where I can.' Johan grinned at Jannus. '"Sacerdotal duties," they used to call them, or so I do believe, at least.' At this, the vagabond laughed out loud (giving the fold-out chair beneath him a moment of uncertainty), and Jannus found himself laughing along.

'It's not that I don't miss some of what I remember, son,' Johan admitted. 'I used to be quite a film buff; horror movies in particular. You like those?' Jannus nodded.

'There are many bad ones, but the *good* ones just make your spine tingle, and look over your shoulder, though you never even seen the monster, oh dear.' Johan slapped a scarred hand on his knee. 'Of course, there's a lot of silly stuff as well; all those people going outside to investigate when they hear something suspicious. Silly stuff I tell you.' Johan looked pointedly at Jannus. 'Especially, since the *real* danger is almost always *inside,* eh son?'

Jannus found himself agreeing with the old man; he almost asked for the can of beer he had, at first, refused, but somehow, he thought it would ruin this moment.

'Oh, and *music.* How I adored music. Jazz and classical music in particular, different in tradition though they might be.' Jannus thought the vagabond was tearing up again at his own memories.

'I've long forgotten his name, son, yet there was one composer, I *truly* adored. The way he could express the heart and soul of man was definitely unique.

Sometimes I still hum his melodies, even if his name escapes me.'

Jannus felt that the moment to leave the vagabond was almost upon him. Yet this chance meeting in this brown and golden field felt somewhat profound to him. *Special.* He felt an uncommon urge to give the old man something back, though he was unsure what exactly it was he felt the old man had given *him.*

'Thank you, Johan,' he managed to begin. The vagabond looked at him, not saying anything, apparently content to let Jannus take his time, after his own tale. 'I think I learned something here, though I'm not sure what exactly.' Jannus thought he saw the old man smiling slightly under the beard, yet he remained silent. 'My own road seems uncertain, but I think I might be on to something here. Finally, you know?'

'Aye, son, I think I might just.' And then Johan of the Outer Isles laughed out loud. Dumbfounded, Jannus looked at the old man, not understanding. Then, after a few moments, started to laugh himself, first as a low chuckle, then rising almost to a primal roar.

'Well, I guess you just might, Johan,' he said, and reached out his hand to the vagabond. Johan grasped his hand with a firm grip, sure and steady, and looked Jannus straight in the eye.

'I hope you find what you want on this road of yours, my boy. I truly do. It might not be what you thought it was going to be, and it might not even make sense, at first. So long that it is *you* that made the decision to walk this road, it cannot be all bad.' Johan released his grip. 'I'll not give you any advice, son, even though I'd mean it well if I did. But I'll say this; no matter what road, no matter what choice, you'll not succeed without some *regret*. You think you might make it without, and I really hope you do. Just don't be *too* surprised if it's not all bliss. Okay, son?'

Somehow, Jannus found himself trusting Johan of the Outer Isles, though he had only met the man mere minutes ago. Thus, he found himself telling the vagabond of his destination, which, curiously, made the man guffaw, almost falling off his seat again.

'Ah son, then you're on quite the journey, following this path!' Johan chuckled, beer in hand. '*There* is your destination, friend.' Jannus looked at where the man pointed, and then looked back at him, not understanding.

'You're moving straight west, boy, if you follow this trail behind me.' Jannus looked behind Johan and where he had set up his camp, and could not find anything resembling a 'trail'. He had walked this way through the wild terrain, expecting it would lead him faster toward his goal.

Johan explained otherwise. 'Moving this way, you'll reach the coastal town of Newport, eventually. The vagabond shook his head. 'Strange folk there, I heard'. Then he chuckled again. 'But then, they might say the same thing of Johan of the Outer Isles, eh?' He smiled at Jannus, who returned the gesture.

'Nay, my friend, you can find your way back to the high road, which will take you north-east at first, before it turns back west.' Johan took a great gulp from his beer. Jannus judged that one gulp almost half-emptied the can. 'Or,' the vagabond resumed his directives. 'You can cross the land adjusting your direction a bit, *north*-west.'

Jannus wanted to protest that he *had* been moving in exactly that direction, then decided not to; Johan, a man of the roads and the land was assuredly correct. 'The land begins to rise to the north-west, my friend,' Johan told him. 'It rises, and eventually you will find your forest on its hill.'

The vagabond's words made Jannus remember; his home town was surrounded by the great waters to the west, and its three high hills sheltering it from the landside. Jannus considered for a few moments, and then took off his backpack, and rummaged through it, while Johan looked on.

Finally, Jannus found what he was looking for; a few of his supplies, and the bottle of liquor. With a word of thanks, he handed both to the vagabond, who tipped his cap, eyes almost twinkling. Jannus nodded at the old man, gave a final thanks, and returned to his chosen path. He had turned around quickly, so that the vagabond would not see the beginning of tears on his face. And Johan of the Outer Isles was left to minister his own roads that he had chosen to walk so many years ago.

CHAPTER XIII

In the Name of Ingratitude

It was the second night under the stars since Jannus had left his home behind. The sky was orange-red and clear. One of the benefits of leaving the city behind was that the sky was not obscured or veiled by all the city-lights. You did not really notice that, when inside the city-limits; only by leaving, and travelling beyond the borders did you see.

Jannus had been nearing the forest for a while — now walking in the *correct* direction. He had ascended the rising hill until he stood before his childhood forest. He felt exhausted, yet not necessarily in a bad way. It felt different to, say, waking up in the middle of the night from a dreamscape, or hungover, maybe, where he would also wake up sweating, and exhausted. This was different. He was tired, yes, but he also felt kind of… good.

Jannus had made a make-shift camp at the edge of the forest. Though the forest was somewhat limited in scope, he did not want to enter it at night-time. Not that he was fearful or anything; he just did not want the extra hassle of trying to traverse through the heavy undergrowth. His self-made camp was — yet again — pretty poor: he used his backpack as a sort of head-neck-back support, and had removed his jacket to sit on a small patch of gold. This night felt colder than the one before, but he did not have the means of making a fire. Even if he did, Jannus was unsure if he was even able to make it work: he had never been the most practical of men. No one had really taught him those skills at otherwise opportune times. He remembered a certain time in the pleasance with his father.

His father, the mighty Mr Rubens, did not often share much of anything with his offspring; well, not Jannus, at least. Though only a child at the time, Jannus had been painfully aware that whenever his father shared anything emotional, he had usually been in his cups. So it had been in the pleasance with its flower recesses and nesting holes.

'Boy!' his father had almost shouted at him. Apparently his father had called for him for a while, since his voice had kept rising until it got the attention it so craved. His mother's soft knock at the door to Jannus' room had revealed that most frail woman (with that most silent strength), who had urged her son along with a frightened nod of the head toward the pleasance.

'You're late, boy!' his father had almost shouted when he had seen him. Boy-Jannus had not looked his father in the eyes a lot, and not this time, either. They had been frightening to behold; a pale, blue stare that fixed you wherever you stood, almost paralytic and unremorseful.

'Your mother tells me that you're not performing well at school, again? Is that true, boy?' Little Jannus had only nodded, flinching slightly when he had seen his fathers' shiny black shoes enter his line of vision. 'There's no excuses that I know, so do not even bother,' his father had proclaimed, all stentorian. Years later, Jannus would imagine that his father had practised that volume and tone of voice in front of his bedroom mirror, until he got it just right.

'Ah, maybe it's partly my fault,' his father had said, and had put a meaty hand on his son's shoulder. Even though Jannus had still not looked up at his father, who had been at least twenty inches taller than his son at that time, Jannus could still smell the wine emanating from his father; some kind of peach, or pear — he had not been a hundred per cent sure. At that specific point in time, Jannus had not yet reached the level of expert and finesse that he would later attain.

'Look at me, boy,' his father had said, still holding a hand on Jannus' shoulder. Looking up, the boy had looked into his father's blood-shot, pale-blue eyes. Though his father had gained quite a few pounds in weight, and his face looked all puffy, he had somehow still retained his forceful presence, at least in his son's eyes. Years would pass yet before Jannus would lose that fearful regard of his pater. He had also realised that his father had laid a hand on his shoulder, not because of any sense of *emotional* support toward his offspring, no: his father was gently swaying, and was holding on to his son for his own need of support. Jannus had begun to feel his father's enormous weight, and was hoping for an early release.

'When I was your age, boy, my father used to take me fishing. He had an old fishing boat, you see; my father was at the helm, and he let me gather up the nets.' Jannus' own father had moved away to sit in chair in a shaded corner of the pleasance. At a nearby table was an empty glass, and a half-full, hatch-cut glass decanter. Jannus had been half disappointed that his father had moved away to something more important to him, and half relieved that his father's shadow had left him.

Sitting down with a heavy thump, his father had filled his glass from the decanter, and pointed a stern finger at his son. 'My father had put out the nets the night before, naturally, yet he let me gather them up, you see, boy?' Jannus had not, but had refrained from speaking up, not seeking further admonition. 'I even helped with the gutting.'

A few minutes of silence had followed after this. His father had apparently forgotten wherever he had been going with his childhood story. After a few mandatory sips, his father had spoken to him, one last time. 'Maybe we should do something like that, Jannus, what do you say? Hmm?'

Surprised, Jannus had only managed to mumble something unintelligible. His father had smiled at him though (yet another surprise), and waved him away again.

A sad memory indeed, Jannus now thought as he looked up at the quiet, starlit sky. The ground underneath him felt cold, but he did not quite freeze. He knew it was coming though; even summer nights in this region were somewhat cool, and him out here without a jacket on. Well, he *had* a jacket with him, of course, but right at the moment it was serving him in a different fashion. *As ever, I take on life's challenges head-on without much planning,* Jannus thought wryly, turning this way and that, trying to find a more comfortable position on jacket and ground. A futile endeavour, of course.

He turned around and opened his backpack. After a bit of searching, Jannus found one of his thick wool sweaters. He *had* remembered something right after all. Usually, it had been his former wife's job to plan their travels, after Jannus had bungled it up more than once. When he had found a slightly more comfortable position, and he felt somewhat warmer, Jannus looked up again at the night sky, and another memory returned to him.

A boy of seven, turning eight, coming home from summer camp. The boy 'knows' that he has been sent away not to enjoy himself, but because he is 'in the way.' He does not know exactly why, but the fact frightens him, anyway. If the boy had had his way, he would have stayed at the camp; every mile and minute he gets closer, his anxiety rises until it almost envelopes him, not like a comforting blanket or duvet, but like something is smothering him, and is leaving him gasping desperately for air.

Yet there is no release. He has to come home. The great family mansion looms from its cliffside, ready to welcome one of its children. When he enters the living room, something is different: toy soldiers are lined up, on the tables, on the window-sills, and even in the bookcase at the far wall. A welcome-home gift? The boy does not feel happy, somehow, though he has expressed his wish for exactly these very toy soldiers. The boy knew he had to pretend to be happy, or else he would be called spoilt, or maybe something worse.

But along with the pretend smile he would feel something else. He would only later understand the meaning. The gift had not been enough for the boy; not enough to re-establish whatever had been lost between him and his parents. The mistrust was just too deep, even then.

'Does courtesy and valour still prevail in the world?' Shocked, Jannus almost jumped to a standing position, and hurt his ankle in the process. 'Mielle?'

Confused (and hurt), Jannus looked around him; he was still at the edge of the forest, at his little make-shift camp; the night sky still starlit. 'Did I fall asleep?'

Feeling groggy, Jannus looked again, almost bewildered. *Maybe I did fall asleep?* He had been exhausted after all, after his up-hill excursions. He looked questioningly at Mielle, who only gazed back at him silently. Jannus thought something was different about her. For one, she wore a dark-green, hooded cloak, rather than her usual amethyst attire. And secondly, and more abstractly, she also seemed 'fuller', somehow. Before, she had always looked somewhat pale and ghostly. 'As if in a dream,' he muttered, and then, 'Courtesy and valour?' he asked her, kneeling down to ascertain the damage done to his ankle.

Looking down at him, she still maintained her regal façade; Jannus got the sensation that Mielle was used to looking down at people, though not necessarily in an altogether bad way.

'What do you mean, Mielle?'

She kept looking at him, a soft smile playing at the corner of her mouth. 'I was calling to you, yet you kept staring up in the dark night, as if unaware of my presence. Or mayhap ignoring me?' Something in her tone, made Jannus want to apologise for his transgressions. Feeling anxiety rising, he accidently bit his cheek, then cursed himself. At least now he forgot about his ankle for a little bit. Mielle was watching him with what he though was mild amusement, yet Jannus thought he could detect just a hint of nervousness on her part, as well.

'I was asleep, Mielle,' he managed. She looked at him curiously, and now Jannus was certain: she *was* nervous. But what for?

Mielle frowned, looked at him, and then herself. She looked at her pale, white hands, and even took hold of her dark-green cloak at the sleeves. Then she looked at Jannus again. 'Maybe you did, Jannus.' She seemed to hesitate, still handling her new cloak. 'Or maybe just lost in thought?'

Jannus shook his head, yet said nothing. He wondered what this particular dreamscape was about. It was not quite like it had been before. It had the same *realness* to it that the dreamscapes usually had, that normal dreams did not manage. He looked around and then up; the sky looked purple and black, yet it also retained strips of orange-red. Did it mean anything?

At the edge of the forest, Jannus suddenly felt scared; he realised he was not certain whether this was real, or one of his most realistic dreamscapes.

'I was thinking about something from when I was a kid, Mielle. Sad thoughts, you know?'

She nodded absently, and looked behind Jannus, at the forest. 'I do not recognise this place, Jannus. Though it does feel… *ancient.* Maybe you brought us here, this time?'

Jannus thought Mielle seemed uncertain, both in manner and words. It made him uncomfortable somehow, uncertain. 'Maybe.' He caressed his cheek, his ankle now almost forgotten. Suddenly it dawned on him. 'I'm hurt, Mielle! I can hurt. Or feel pain, I mean.'

'As I told you before, Jannus, the nature of these places are mostly unknown.' Mielle turned around from her inspection of the edge of the forest, and looked at him again. It took only a moment for her to realise the implications. 'Hurt in a dream? Unusual, yes?'

Jannus folded his arms, feeling the night's chill. 'Very unusual, Mielle', he said, almost petulantly. He did not know why Mielle had a certain way about her that made him feel like a child again. Then again, she did seem kind of *ancient*, in her own way. Not to give voice to that epitaph in her presence, of course. Or even mention the word 'epitaph' for that matter. *Stop fooling around, Jannus,* he told himself, in a mix of his own and his grandmother's voice.

'No, you're not supposed to get hurt in a dream, Mielle. It *should* not be possible.' He thought about that statement, and then corrected himself. 'Of course, it is now known that people *can* hurt themselves while sleepwalking, or maybe hurt an extremity if, say, there is something near where you're sleeping that you hit with said extremity.' He looked at her with an almost desperate look in his eyes. 'But these dreams are different, Mielle. Different to the rest of them'.

Mielle turned her full regal gaze upon him, and as always, he found hope in that confident regard. She smiled. 'Of course, Jannus. Now I gather the importance of your words, and the object of your worry.' She frowned. 'And yet, you spoke of thoughts of a sad nature?'

Jannus found himself telling Mielle of his childhood memories, both to relieve himself of their emotional weight, but also as a sort of distraction. Telling the story, the inner turmoil did not go away, nor those automatic intruders in his mind that always came back unwanted. They were never invited, yet somehow they found a way to his door. And sometimes Jannus even opened the door for them, and let them roam about his house. The old NWFs as he liked to call them. His "Never Welcome Friends". At one point he had even considered coining that abbreviation, but he had never got around to it. Jannus also shared *why* he was even here; of his wish to go home. Still feeling ambivalent about how much he should share with her, Jannus withheld the detail of the letter in his pocket. 'I need to go home, Mielle. Something awaits me there.'

Mielle had listened to his story in silent contemplation, with her head at a soft angle, not looking directly at him, but at some place just beyond him. It was a rare gift she had. They stood there for a while, under the starlit, night sky, at the forest's edge, listening to the sounds from within. Something rustled, and something else cracked. Something flapped, and something else hissed. As a child, all these sounds had evoked fanciful imagery, yet now, as an adult, full of anxiety and negative energy, the images had turned to shadow, hiding monsters deep within; not the monsters of childhood, but those spawned from an adult mind.

His thoughts turned back to Johan, who had seemed to be in quietude, when Jannus had left him. He wondered what the minister of the roads would have made of Mielle; if they would ever meet. For the first time since he had made her acquaintance, Jannus felt a sliver of distrust. Somehow, comparably, the story of Johan of the Outer Isles, felt altogether more… *truthful.*

'Which carries the greater weight, Jannus? Deep human loyalty or the inevitable moral imperative?' Mielle interrupted his musings in her usual imperial manner. Jannus turned to her. She had taken her first few steps inside the shadowed forest. Again, he thought her behaviour was markedly different to before; much more hesitant and unsure of herself, despite her regal speech being almost the same.

'Moral imperatives, my lady?' he asked her, preferring a neutral path forward. Most people, Jannus knew, would probably consider him somewhat abstruse. And that was, admittedly, partly by design. It was just a way of keeping most people at a distance. And it had proved effective to a certain extent, at least in the short-term range. Looking back, it had proved to have more negative consequences than intended. Mielle, however, seemed to have no issue in ascertaining his shallow motives.

'Do you cling to the past, Jannus? Or do you find a way forward, despite the hardships? The sufferings endured? Do shadows haunt you, Jannus? Follow your every step, as if they never left in the first place?' She stepped closer. This time, he noticed there was no hesitance to her movements. And even though he was a head taller than her, Jannus still felt that she was the imposing one. *It's the eyes,* he told himself, as they stood partway in shadow. *Most of it is in the eyes. I never learned that.*

Mielle put on hand on his shoulder. She did not have to stand on her toes to reach him, but it was somewhat of a stretch for her. 'We all carry shadow in our hearts, dear one. They never leave, and nor should we want them to.' Her hand felt soft on his shoulder, yet it seemed to carry an immense weight to it. It did not drain him of vitality with its great weight, but rather seemed to infuse him with some strange and savage strength. He felt the inner turmoil lessen, though it did not go away completely. And the intrusive thoughts were still there, yet now they seemed to just complain amongst themselves, which *was* an annoyance, to be sure, but preferable to the alternative. Another detail then struck him: Mielle's hand on his shoulder had also felt *real*. Jannus was unsure if they had ever actually made physical contact before in his visions, or if they had, consciously or otherwise, kept out of each other's proximity. Maybe this was the changing nature of the dreamscape that Mielle had spoken of?

'See these shadows before us, Jannus?' He nodded, looking inside the forest from its very edge, remembering the time when it had worked both as a place of wonder, and a sanctuary. 'This is our path. Through the shadows of past and future, both. This is our way.' She looked at him, smiling reassuringly, and he found himself returning the smile, despite his misgivings. 'Focus on the path you want to thread, Jannus. These places can take you where you *need* to go. Where one *must* go. Through the dream we can find your destination. There is *power* in these places, Jannus; *energy* that may help us on our way. Focus on your heart's desire.'

Jannus picked up his jacket from ground, and dusted it off before putting it on. And with his backpack back in its usual spot, Mielle led him by the hand into the woods of the past, with the starlit night sky above bearing witness, as they disappeared from sight.

CHAPTER XIV

Esprit de Corps

'Damnation.'

Mielle was complaining again. Jannus made sure to uphold a straight face; the lady of the ghost realms had been having trouble with the heavy underbrush in the woods. Just a few minutes ago she had almost tripped, and made a selection of curses, most unbefitting a lady of high birth. Jannus had laughed out loud, unable to contain himself. Mielle had turned and looked around, glaring at him. She had further explained to him the nature of the dreamworld; how time sometimes worked differently here, and that they might be able to *interact* more with their surroundings. 'Though not everywhere and not always without consequences,' she had warned. To his amusement, Mielle seemed to have her own difficulties, traversing through the woods. Once or twice, he had not managed to contain his laughter.

This time he held his composure, and looked to his own safety, and where to tread. He could feel her gaze though. After a while he could hear her continue onwards, muttering under her breath. Jannus himself had not been completely unharmed; he had several small cuts on his forearms from when he had tried to remove some branches with hidden thorns. Even his jeans had a single cut across the shin. Mielle had not said anything when he had cried out about that, but Jannus could have *sworn* that he had felt her smile. He was still surprised *why* he could be hurt here, and wondered at the implications.

Worse than all of this, though, were his growing anxieties. Just a while earlier, Mielle had asked for water, and he had opened his backpack to provide her with one of the cans of spring water he had been so fortunate to pack. Suddenly he realised, all over again, that he had forgotten to pack his medicines. For a moment he had even craved the bottle of liquor he had given to Johan of the Outer Isles. Jannus still felt somewhat ambivalent about that; on the one hand, he felt like he might need it himself. On the other, he felt guilty giving it to the vagabond. Would the bottle really help Johan? Part of Jannus wished that maybe the vagabond would end up giving it away to someone else.

In the not-too-distant past, whenever Jannus had lacked a sufficient stash of his liquid or synthesised support, his mind would be assaulted by a flood of automatic derivates, and his pulse would gather in strength. It would be as if the ground underneath cracked, and he drowned under the dirt and rubble.

And as he had followed Mielle through the forest, he had felt his old worries and doubts and anxieties rising, augmented a great deal by his current circumstances.

Is all this real?
What are you going to do?
Something bad is going to happen
You're never going to succeed
What are you even trying to do?
Just give up
Does this even matter?
Is it even real?
Am I alone?
Was I always?

Somehow the former therapist had managed to contain a respectable veneer, despite the emotional and cognitive barrage. Even Mielle did not seem to have noticed anything, being mostly concerned with her own wonder with the forest. In a distant part of his mind, Jannus had wondered if, perhaps, she had never had any experience being in a forest before. Somehow, he imagined not. He could see her attending balls and other high social gatherings; he could see her at court, dispensing justice, high and low. She *had* remarked though, that she knew the forest was ancient.

Along with the emotional and mental assault, there had been a series of disturbing images.

A child's face hidden behind broken bones, almost like a mask; a daystar above, low in the sky. A boy with a pencil, drawing eternal realms of black shadow and deep purple.

Two rows of stones, small in size, forming an oval,

and two sticks; one placed vertically, the other at a forty-five-degree angle from the first one. Half a skull of a bird of prey lying in the stone circle, around it something unidentifiable, putrescent.

A cave on a hill, halfway to the summit, something predacious on the hunt, sure of its scent, taloned feet submerged in the ground, in the flesh.

A circle of bones showing the way to the land of the dead, a comedy beyond measure.

All of this had flashed through his mind in mere seconds, yet he was still feeling the effects of it. They had wandered through the woods, Mielle in the lead, yet Jannus directing the path from his childhood memories.

He was surprised at how much he remembered from this place, yet many boyhood hours had been spent here, after all, escaping the dreaded reality of family life. This place had felt more real, in a way, or at least it had been a place where there had been more room for *him*. Maybe this was why it had remained to crystallise in his memory…

For many years, Jannus had tried to remain unperturbed by most things, preferring a comfortable detachment from real-life events. He had never seemed to care about the things that most people cared about.

'Your boy is extraordinarily obtuse, Mr and Mrs Rubens,' one of his teachers had declared to his parents, at one of the obligatory parent-teacher meetings. 'He's bright enough, sure, yet *he does not seem to care very much.*'

Well, that that been true enough. At least, with regard to whatever people around him were telling him to do. In his own eyes, Jannus had never been obtuse; not as a child, nor as an adult. In his own view, he had made the necessary arrangements to abstain from a world that had been out to hurt him. So he had taken precautions, and made his plans. He had fortified, and secured the battlements. And he had led his life, mostly safely, and paid the price. Again, and again.

'Reminiscing again, Jannus?' a voice called, ahead of him. Jannus looked up. There was a small opening in the tree-crowns; it looked to be early in the morning, though time was difficult to tell here, as Mielle had hinted. The sky was brightening, and the day-life of the forest was beginning to dominate the soundscape.

'Oh, I was just thinking about my time here as a child, you know,' Jannus answered, carefully. 'This place was sort of a haven for me back then.'

'A refugium of the soul, mayhap?' Mielle asked. Walking ahead of him, she deftly avoided a couple of snapping branches that she had pushed aside. She *was* getting better at this, Jannus noticed.

For himself though, the forest had lost some its childhood wonder, its magic lustre. He had no difficulty in traversing or navigating through it, yet it took him a while to ascertain why. The forest was a lot more structured than he remembered; the pathways much more direct, and clean. And there were *signs* everywhere, describing the wildlife, and information arrows directing people to where they needed to go. There was no danger in getting lost. He had pointed out one of the signs to Mielle. 'Sometimes we see what we expect, remember?' she had answered him. 'Dreams and reality are entwined in ways we cannot fully explain.'

'Sort of,' Jannus now said, following one of the correct arrows. 'I would go here once in a while, when things got... heated. Back home.' Ahead of him, he could see brightness, which most likely meant the other edge of the forest — unless they had hit upon a clearing, or something. The information was pretty accurate though, so in a few minutes' time they should hit upon the other edge of the forest. It was not that he *wanted* to get lost, exactly; nor wanted to get into any dangerous situation. Yet something had clearly been lost through all those years; the woods had lost their wildness and their mystery, and had now succumbed to the modern reality with all its narrow pathways.

'Ah I see,' Mielle said, picking up pace; maybe she had seen the light ahead as well, and was eager to head out. In fact, Jannus found it hard to keep up with her, even though it was his old stomping ground they were traversing. She was muttering something unintelligible, and only a few of her words reached back to him.

'Pale shadows of dragons, they came back to us, did they not? Broken ramparts, betrayal of promised shields, they came back.'

Jannus wished he understood her better than he did.

Real dragons? Truly? Part of him was afraid that he might be losing his mind: when he had set out a couple of mornings ago, he had been sort of excited and expectant of what his journey would bring him. It had seemed like a new beginning in a way; or at least, the *promise* of one.

Now, he had become more anxious in terms of being here. Was he dreaming, or was this real? When he had set out, it seemed real enough, until last night when Mielle had appeared in his dreamscape to be his guide once again. He had followed her as he had previously. But something was different this time around. She seemed too real, somehow. And it looked like their roles had changed to some extent: Jannus himself had assumed the role of guide, at least through this part of the dreamscape.

On the other hand, *dragons?* The other part of him — the hidden childhood part — wanted that part to be *more* real. *Now, are they going to be of the chromatic sort, or the metallic sort?* As a child he had feared the former, and been appropriately respectful of the latter.

Mielle had stopped by a pond. Jannus could not remember it being here, but maybe this was a different part of the woods, where he had never ventured, or maybe it was part of the dreamscape. Mielle had knelt down by the edge of it. Jannus kept a few steps behind her. It did not look as though she was doing anything; she seemed to just stare at the water, but he noticed that there were constant ripples, as if someone kept throwing in stones.

'This place, reminds me...' Mielle started, then felt silent again. Jannus listened to the sounds of the woods around him, while he waited for Mielle to continue.

'I heard tales of a man once, Jannus — a pilgrim. How old he was, I do not know: the stories do not say. He had been travelling from place to place, spreading the word, and the truth. He travelled only with a small collection of scrolls, whereupon he had written all that he had seen. And through his words, the people came to know about each other, and their different ways. He showed them a light in their darkness, a way out of the shadows. He wanted no followers, no power. And yet still he held sway, wherever his word had been heard. And then one day, he made one last journey — to where, no one knows. Some say he journeyed to the ends of the world, and maybe beyond, while others spoke of him becoming a ruler of great nations. I have even heard hushed whispers about him dying alone in the dark, regretting all of his words.'

Mielle stood up at the edge of the pond as she finished her tale. Jannus thought she appeared exhausted after telling that story, but he could not be certain. He reached out a hand in comfort, then stayed his hand.

'I do not know why I remembered that story, Jannus,', she said, softly. He noticed that the ripples in the pond had stopped. *Someone had stopped throwing stones, maybe? What a foolish thought!*

'What do you think happened to the pilgrim, Mielle?'

She had kept looking into the pond as if some truth were hidden in there. Finally, she looked at him with a sad smile. 'I do not know, Jannus. Yet I hope he found his peace wherever he journeyed. We cannot wish for more.'

Jannus had nothing to say to that. Mielle turned around, and he followed along. Even the woods themselves seemed silent. After a short while, Jannus noticed that the forest seemed to get brighter, and up ahead, what looked to be morning light shone through the trees. They had reached the other edge of the forest.

'Wait, Jannus.' He turned around. Mielle had stopped, and appeared to be looking around in search of something. She seemed to sense his curiousness. 'Certain places have a certain *energy* to them, Jannus. Remember?' He nodded. 'There are… *thresholds*… or borders and barriers, where it is possible to…' Mielle appeared to struggle with her words.

A thought occurred to Jannus. 'Can you follow then, my lady?' She looked at him, puzzled, then understanding dawned on her. 'Aye, Jannus. Though, not without consequence.' Then suddenly, she tilted her head, and smiled.

'What it is, Mielle?' he asked. 'Something wrong?'

'Nay, Jannus,' she said absently, taking steps towards an ancient pine tree. She reached into the underbrush just at the eastern side of it. 'There!' she exclaimed, and stood up with a great stick in both hands. It was about six feet long (taller than her, slightly shorter than Jannus himself), and about three inches wide, from what he could see. It was unsharpened at either end, yet it looked like someone had taken a knife to begin carving, as it was missing a chunk of its bark in the middle of it. The wood looked to be pine: maybe it had fallen off from its parent above. *Or broken off,* Jannus thought. Though he could not explain why, he was somehow disturbed by this finding.

Mielle seemed pleased though. 'Look Jannus, this will help to support our traversing, I am sure of it.'

'Do you need such, my lady?' He could not help but tease her. She did not answer, but Jannus thought he could spy a slight twitch at the corner of her mouth, as if she held back a grin. It was difficult to tell though. From what he knew of her so far, Mielle appeared to be somewhat in control of her expressions. They walked together, out of the woods.

His hometown was visible in the distance. It was situated in a coastal valley area, with hills rising on three sides of it. On the western side was the ocean, stretching as far as his child's eyes could imagine. The edge of the forest on this side was right beside the bottom of one such hill. It was still early morning, and the sky was clear. The hillside was full of cotton grass and poppies, dryas and dusky-winged fritillaries. He did not remember any of those being there while he was there. But then, he was but a child, and did not possess any acuity concerning the local flora. Or maybe it was the nature of the dreamscape, that things appeared here that he half-remembered from several places in the real-life, and his mind messed the whole thing up. Made it all a jumble, and maybe even senseless.

A water stream was gently bubbling down the side of the nearest hill, and almost right beside it, halfway up to the summit, was an old, dilapidated, red-brown shed. He remembered *that* at least. The rumours among the kids at the time was that a crazy old man was living there. The stories about him gave more than one explanation of *why* he was crazy, one even more outlandish than the last. Some of them had even been contradictory, though that had never made the story-tellers (or the audience) hesitate. All the times that Jannus had passed that red-brown shed as a child, no one had ever stepped out of that door to chase him, or shout him away.

'This was the place of your birth?' Mielle asked, standing beside him.

He nodded. 'Yes, there it is, in all its glory.' She frowned at him, and he recognised the sarcastic tone of his voice. 'Well, not exactly the place of my birth. But I grew up here.' He pointed to the hill opposite their current position. 'You can even see my boyhood home from here. *There,* just a bit up the hillside, the great white mansion? It stands a bit apart from the rest of it.'

It took a few seconds for Mielle to see it, and then she made an affirmative gesture; it looked to Jannus as if she had regained her regal composure, having been out of her element in the woods.

'Ah yes, I see it Jannus. *There*, the one with the dark roofing?' He nodded. She smiled at him. 'It even has a *pleasance?*'

Part of him wondered, *how can she see that from here?* And also, *why did that make her smile*? Jannus again wished that he had a better understanding of her. Whenever he had asked a question about her, of a personal nature, she had deflected him with apparent ease. He had assumed Mielle was not real, or at least only real in the sense that his dreamscapes had any resemblance to reality.

This close to his childhood home, with all its wonder and terror, things were beginning to unravel for Jannus; the frail threads of his sanity exposed. He felt his anxiety rising, and was failing to regain his composure, and balance. And all the negative and automatic was on a rise, ready to begin its assault, sensing his weakness, his moment of faltering. He almost felt his knees buckle, when a gentle hand touched his arm.

'Steady, Jannus,' he heard her voice. *Is she real?* 'Your heart must remain strong, dear one. When past and present meet, the human mind is always assailed, Jannus. In such moments, we show our mettle.' He felt her hand tense. 'A shield must not waver. Not again.'

And while the daystar slowly made its way to its inevitable apotheosis, Mielle and Jannus left the forest behind them, as the mansion on the hill got ready to welcome home its long-lost son.

CHAPTER XV

Under an Obsidian Sky

They were heading down the hill when they suddenly heard a sound behind them. Mielle and Jannus turned around at almost the same time. Mielle held the stick in front of her, almost like a weapon — maybe a quarterstaff of sorts. They looked at each other; Jannus held an index finger before his lips. *Quiet now.* Mielle nodded in understanding, keeping her silence, stick in front of her. Jannus thought he heard something shuffling behind the shed, and then it was silent again.

Curiosity got a hold of him, and he moved a few steps closer to the shed. It had a single, small-framed window on this side, yet it was so dirty you could not see anything through it. Jannus stopped, listening again. He thought he heard something whimpering.

'Anybody there?' he called out, a small part of him wishing he had the stick instead of Mielle, a few steps behind him.

There was no answer from behind the shed, only silence. Then, as Jannus was preparing to turn around again, a dog came walking slowly toward them. Jannus quickly dispelled the notion that the dog might somehow be feral or dangerous; it looked tense, yes, but clearly, it was more scared of them than the other way around. Or so he thought, anyway.

'Jannus, you must maintain your distance from this beast!' He looked around at her, in wonder. She had assumed a defensive position, keeping her eyes on the sad creature that slid closer and closer to Jannus.

'Don't worry, Mielle,' he tried to calm her. 'This one means no harm, I'm sure.' She did not lower the staff, and Jannus had the thought that Mielle seemed proficient in the use of it, somehow.

The dog was a collie, Jannus saw. Or maybe a border-collie: he did not know the difference. It seemed harmless enough, really. The dog sniffed his outstretched hand a few times, and tried a lick or two. Apparently, this was enough for Jannus to gain the dog's trust, as the latter began panting, and pawing at the ground.

Jannus grinned at Mielle, who had still not moved from her initial position, though she *had* lowered the stick just a few inches. 'It's quite all right, my lady,' he said to her. 'As you can see, he's already our friend.'

'Yours maybe,' Mielle muttered, though she *did* shift the stick from a defensive weapon to a walking implement again. *Maybe dogs are wild where she is from,* Jannus wondered, as the collie was now rolling around on the ground, while he rubbed its (his) belly.

'You're a good boy, aren't you? A good boy... Yes, you are,' Jannus found himself talking to the dog.

As a boy himself he had always wanted a dog. Not a collie, but one of those mean guard dogs, maybe. Not as a companion, but more as a protector. He had often imagined what difference it might have made had he had one, growing up.

'*You* wouldn't have been much of a protector, would you, boy?' he now said to the collie on his back in front him, still satisfied by the belly-rub.

'Are you conversing with the creature, Jannus?' he heard Mielle say behind him, incredulously. Jannus almost burst with laughter at both her question and tone, before he composed himself. Luckily, he was half-sitting with his back to her.

'No, Mielle,' he managed. 'Just trying to calm it down, you know?'

Jannus could not see a dog-tag of any sort, so no contact-information either. This particular hill was as yet unpopulated, unlike the other two, where they had begun building private houses a while ago. Jannus did not know why this hill remained almost empty. Maybe because it was close to the forest? *No that does not make sense,* he thought.

Standing, the collie looked up at him expectantly, still panting.

'We have to go boy, you understand?' Jannus was unsure of his own reaction, having to leave the dog behind. As a young adult he had completely dropped the notion of getting a dog, or any sort of pet, really. Too much time and work, too much care and responsibility.

'What is that marking there, Jannus? On the creature's haunches?'

Interrupted in his musings, he looked at the place she had pointed out. The fur of the collie was a mixture of white on the belly and chest, and fire-red in the face, as well as on the back and its sides. On its right haunch though, there was a red-golden mark. The only association Jannus had of the shape of it was of a bishop's crozier, with two serpents intertwining at the crown. As he reached out to touch it, the dog stepped back, and growled at him. Not aggressively in the manner of getting ready to attack, yet just enough to give a warning. *Curious,* Jannus thought.

'I saw such a marking once,' Mielle revealed, finally getting closer to the collie and Jannus. The former stopped its growling, and started to wag its tail, and pant at her approach. Mielle looked at the dog suspiciously, not letting down her guard completely.

'Truly?' he asked her, looking at the mark again.

'Aye. We were walking through the golden grass fields, Jannus. I remember walking by a father with his two half-grown sons with hair the colour of their father, eyes of their deceased mother, all three in shadow, looking at the daystar through burning flame.'

Mielle looked at Jannus. 'Why do I remember them like that, do you think?' Almost feeling guilty for not knowing how to reply, Jannus was relieved when she did not wait for an answer. 'You could see the mountain from the graveside, where they waited for the procession to reach us. The dual serpent coming to visit, Jannus. A great honour it was, truly. I saw him first from a distance before his full glory came to embrace us. He walked with a great staff, taller than himself, embedded with such a crown.' Mielle pointed at the dog, who sniffed in her general direction, then resumed his ever-important panting.

'I saw him near the entrance to the Fallen Hold, with the architrave above, depicting "The Descent of Night." Mielle sounded simultaneously proud, and saddened. Even the collie gave off a mournful whimper at this revelation. 'He did not appear as a creature of great strength and aggression, but seemed rather timid and somnolent.' Mielle looked to both Jannus and the collie, almost as if she wanted to be reassured, Jannus thought. 'Did we deserve so fine a guest, Jannus? We had made preparations, banners and flags, the children with flowers in their hair. And then the skies had darkened above us leaving no remorse. There had been no enmity. Did we do the wrong thing?'

Again, Jannus did not know the answer. As a child, he had maintained his sense of wonder, and mystery; as an adult, he seemed to have repudiated such phenomena. It had been replaced by critical thinking and analytical study. Not that he now disparaged such things, but he had begun to mourn the absence of the child-like sense of the magical. *My above-neck cynicism,* he thought wryly.

It seemed to be on a return now, though he was

unsure if it was a manner of natural progression, mental instability, or something else entirely. A deviation? Whatever it was, Jannus was sure that he could learn something from this experience, whatever its foundation. He looked at Mielle. *She suddenly appeared to him as someone, who had lost everything.* The collie had stepped closer to Mielle, and licked her hand a few times. Mielle did not say anything, or retreat, but only smiled sadly.

Jannus felt sad, too.

CHAPTER XVI

A Post-War Dream?

As they continued to descend the eastern hills, his home town got closer and closer. Jannus wished that he had a better view of it, but it seemed like the closer they got, his vision became blurred, as if the town were enveloped in thick mist. Or maybe it was himself? When Jannus had remarked on his blurred vision to Mielle, she had only frowned at him.

'My vision remains clear, Jannus,' she had told him.

And so she had become his eyes during the descent. She told him what she saw. She spoke of a great red building in a rectangle with a black roof, which could only be the town's public school. Another one, west of the school, almost as large, but blue in colour, had to be the community centre. She told him of the white building with spires (the church), and of a large collection of square buildings, 'high, dull and grey' (the industrial area). In his mind's eye, Jannus could recollect most of it. She also spoke of things unknown to him; the way Mielle described it, it sounded like his home town had expanded quite a bit, since he had made his home here. It sounded like a city proper, to his reluctant surprise.

The industrial ward had been off-limits for him and his friends, which had just made it all the more exciting to enter those grounds. He had never told his parents of these excursions, and he did not suspect they knew of it. His grandmother had, though.

'Been off-course again, Jan?' she would ask him with a knowing look in her eyes. Jannus always suspected his grandmother of having visited those off-limit areas back in her own childhood days. 'Whenever you see a keep-off sign, Jannus,' she had once told him, just a short time before her passing, 'just take a few steps on the grass. Just try it, Jannus. Just to keep your sanity'. It had taken him a few years and some eclectic music experiences to understand the reference.

Their descent was mostly in silence. Mielle seemed preoccupied with her own thoughts, and Jannus was experiencing an increasing dread. They were very close to their destination now. The descent was not going to last forever. Paradoxically, he was also growing increasingly annoyed that most of his vision of his home town remained in mist. *Maybe part of me was looking forward to seeing it again?* The only visible thing so far remained his childhood home; the family mansion high upon its hill above the mist.

The only cheery one in their small party was the collie. He had found a stick of his own that he was playing with joyously; throwing it up in the air, and taking it along for short runs. Jannus found some small amusement by imagining that the collie was mimicking Mielle, still walking with her own stick in hand to support her walk down the hill.

Finally, Mielle broke her silence. 'Curious thing, this town of yours, Jannus.'

'What's so curious about it?' he asked her.

Mielle pointed ahead of her with her make-shift staff. 'I have difficulty ascertaining the nature of the place, Jannus,' she told him.

Ascertaining? 'I'm not sure I follow, Mielle'. He scratched the dog's head when it came trotting alongside him. The collie looked up at him, still with the stick in his mouth.

'It seems full of life and yet so empty, Jannus. Soulless in a way, without *heart.*' Mielle shook her head, and then said, 'I give you my apology, I cannot express myself in a more exacting way.' And then she looked at him, almost shyly. 'And I did not have the intent of diminishing your home, Jannus.'

Jannus made a conciliatory motion toward her, and they continued their descent in their now customary silence. As the land began to flatten out and they got closer to the edge of town, Jannus thought of Mielle's words and found them to be true.

This modern world with its high promises, only a few places left of love and comfort amidst the need for high accomplishment. Where is the room for you, Jannus? When did you get lost? A few flashes of dreamscapes suddenly attacked his waking mind; *a man lighting a smoke in the dark; another man passing by, giving the first one a half-full bottle; and third man in the corner watching them both with a knowing smile, not in menace but in sorrow, a tattoo of a fabled creature on his chest hidden from view (though not from Jannus). Wooden bowls and ladles left in the waste by the wayside; a family long gone, having left in fear and alarm. A shadowed figure on the ice and water with a steel harpoon in hand, ice-picks at its side, ready to make a striking motion.*

Jannus returned to what now passed for reality through the collie's sharp bark. He looked up. They had finally reached the bottom of the hill and were now walking alongside the eastern road that was the main lifeline of his home town, excluding the harbour on the western side, naturally. The mist seemed much thicker here, or else it had just grown in size since their descent. He could see only the marker with the town's name, and the first few buildings along the eastern road leading into town. Jannus knew that this was not the town proper, but would be considered more like the outskirts. There was still half a mile ahead of him before he could say that he was *truly* home.

A strange sound emanated from the mists: a weird sort of rhythm, almost like a pulse. When he moved closer, Jannus identified the sounds. An empty can on piece of string was hanging from a window, rocking gently back and forth in the wind. On the eastern wall on the opposite side of the road, Jannus could see that most of it was covered by a great army-green tarpaulin, that flapped in the wind. Most likely it was covering a broken window or something. The two sounds together made for an odd sort of theme for his homecoming.

'I tried, in them, to inculcate a modicum of decency,' Mielle suddenly said, as she gazed upon the mist-shrouded outskirts of the town. Her voice was almost a whisper. Jannus had noticed that she had begun to show a degree of lassitude. And disconcertingly, it also looked as if she was beginning to lose some of her substance, as though she had been losing weight since their travels together. It was hard to tell as she was clothed in robes, yet when Jannus looked at her from the corner of his eyes, it was as if she sometimes seemed partly transparent, as if not wholly there (or here?) any more. He had not voiced any of his worries to her so far.

'Mielle?'

She did not answer immediately. The collie walked over to her, sat down and looked up at her with a whimper. Absently, she scratched the dog's head. Despite himself, Jannus smiled. It looked as though she was not only getting accustomed to 'the beast', but had started developing a bond of sorts with it.

'He tergiversated whenever I tried to show him a better path, Jannus. The common folk were being punished by molten-leaden cloaks beneath the crowned arches.' As usual, Jannus made a conscious choice not to speak, as he tried to uncloak whatever she was talking about. He really wanted to know what "tergiversated" meant.

'Things were supposed to have been different after the great conflict, you see,' Mielle continued, as she turned toward him. 'Yet the shadowed hearts remained among us, and before we could see, before we could *react,* it was too late.' Jannus was shocked to see a single tear moving down her cheek. Normally, she would keep her regal composure. Maybe something had finally broken through to her, following him along his path.

'I once knew a woman, Jannus,' she began, slowly, and softly. 'A prisoner, she was, in truth. I came to her cell for many nights, hearing her story, and her defence. She was proud and defiant, and never gave any ground. She told of her people's past and glory. How they had *almost* achieved victory. And she described her people's *end,* yet always with the same pride, always defiant. She never raised her voice at all, or screamed, or spat in my eye. She smiled at me, and looked at me in pity. *Pity,* Jannus! How could she? How? As I left her that final night, I wondered, Jannus. I had doubts; fear, even. Yet the High Court had dispensed its Justice, the crime had been clear, honour had been upheld. And I *still* had doubts. Part of me still grieves for what I had to do.'

Mielle's voice trailed off after that. During her story, another tear had made its way down her other cheek, creating parallel lines on her face, creating quite a sorrowful visage, in Jannus' eyes.

Jannus got the sense that Mielle had more to say,

yet she seemed to hesitate. In a strange way, he had begun to feel grateful to her; he was quite insightful concerning his own obstinate nature, despite almost never deviating from it, yet from her guidance and companionship, he had learned a lot. In this way he felt an obligation, of sorts, to help her out with whatever issue she might be struggling.

'As ever, I'm not confident of your meaning, Mielle. Could you please explain?' And then, in a somewhat softer tone, he added, 'You seem troubled.'

Still looking at him, Mielle nodded. 'Aye, Jannus. I am troubled.' She looked down at the collie and smiled. Jannus thought the dog gave her a smile in return. 'Ha! It would seem like the beast has taken a liking to me!'

Jannus was glad to see her demeanour change, but could not refrain from adding, 'The "beast" might have a name, you know.'

Mielle looked at him suspiciously. 'You name your beasts?' She sounded almost incredulous.

'Aye,' he teased. 'Almost all of them, in fact!'

Still looking at him sideways, she scratched the collie on the top of the head again. Jannus had thought about getting a dog after the divorce, just for company and comfort. But he had surmised it would have been too much work, and responsibility. And the latter, at least, he had never been any good at. Or so someone had told him once. A dog might have been good company for some, but not for him. *No more work or conflict or war for me, thank you,* he had raged. Looking now at Mielle and the collie, he thought he might think differently.

'Let us continue onward, Jannus,' Mielle now said. 'There is time yet for explanations, and you shall have them.'

Relieved, yet still curious and worried, Jannus nodded at her, and started walking forwards, past the town marker. Maybe it was only his imagination, yet it felt as though the mist was parting before him. A shout from behind told him it was also *closing* behind him. Jannus turned around.

Mielle and the collie were still standing on the town near the town marker, just outside where the mist seemed to get more solid in shape.

'Is everything all right?' he called.

Mielle looked at him, as if from a great distance. Maybe she could not hear him?

'Jannus!' he heard her calling, though he could not see her lips move. 'It seems like we cannot continue onward together. The shadows are closing again.'

Jannus tried to move forward in the direction of Mielle and the collie, but found he could only take a few steps forward, before *something* stopped him, as if the mist was solid in truth. Solid enough to deny him passage back, anyway.

The last thing he saw before the mists closed the way back completely was Mielle raising her hand. At first, it looked as though she moved, as if in parting; if it was though, it was strange and unknown to him. And then he heard her call for a final time.

'Do not fear, Jannus. When shadows assail your heart, your true courage will show itself.' A few seconds of silence followed. And then, *'You had it all along, Jannus. You carried it with you all the way. You just could not see.'*

Confused, he looked around. He started to walk forwards, in what he thought might be the correct way. *Or maybe I'm just going the only way available to me,* he thought, slightly disconcerted. Jannus used the makeshift quarterstaff for support, through the mists, as he carefully made his way. A few moments later, he looked at the six-foot staff in wonder. 'How did I get that?' he exclaimed, his voice sounding loud, yet lonely in the mist. Did Mielle give it to him before parting? He did not think so.

Feeling somewhat dazed, and shaking his head as if waking from a dream, he continued through the mist, back to his hometown — *city* now, aptly named Euphoria's Edge.

'Ten years gone,' the gentleman of leisure mused. Ten years or more. He had stopped counting here in this old house, now broken or forgotten. 'Myself or the house?' The gentleman had stopped caring long ago about that particular distinction. After getting lost by the wayside after the great conflict, nothing much mattered any more. He shifted his feet on the dirty floor. No one had

cleaned here in quite a while. As the floor was dirty, so were his naked feet. Again, it held no significance any more. In the long-gone days of his childhood, he had not cared about clean feet, either. Other people had, though; he remembered that much. However, clean feet had not prepared him for what was to come. Clean feet had not made him able to resist. He had still succumbed. It did not matter now, though. He just had one more thing to do. All would be revealed. A reckoning.

CHAPTER XVII

Trudging Through the Ashes

At the edge of town, Jannus walked through the mist, half-blind and unsure of himself, able to see only a few feet ahead of himself. He found comfort in the makeshift quarterstaff, that he somehow had found in his possession. Had she given it to him?

It had become increasingly clear to Jannus that he had a choice before him; it was not a question of good and evil, or right and wrong; but another kind of choice. This was his future; this was a way he could truly decide something. Make a difference, even. It was a choice more akin to light and dark: both equally viable, both could be wielded for positive, and negative. Self-supportive, or self-destructive. For years now, he had chosen the latter. Had it been a matter of choice, though? Maybe not completely, yet sufficient for him to start feeling a sense of responsibility. Not only towards himself, but to people around him. Maybe this was his last chance? And how he had *longed* for one such.

Not that there were many left in his life; his sister, of course. His ex-wife, maybe. The old, widowed neighbour? In a sense, yes. Johan of the Outer Isles?

Why not? The collie of uncertain allegiance? Oh, most certainly? And Mielle? Mielle?

No matter his past choices and their outcomes, Jannus felt that he now had another chance, another path to take. With him he brought both light and dark; now was the time to wield both properly. He put a hand in his front pocket, and made sure the letter was still there. It was, secure in its envelope. Several times he had thought to take it out and read it again, maybe show it to Mielle. Maybe she would have had some sort of wisdom or insight as to the content of the letter, or the motivation of its sender. But somehow, he had never managed to bring it up. It was not as if he had forgotten it — not at all. But somehow it had seemed more insignificant in her presence, not worthy of her time. Besides, what could she have known of it? He had never forgotten the presence in his pocket, but now it felt as if it had gained in weight, somehow. Maybe thinking about it made it heavier?

Jannus himself was fairly certain of who the sender had been. Or at least, he had narrowed it down to two or three different people, all former clients of his. And of those three, one in particular stood out. Or rather, when Jannus envisioned the sender, that person remained half-hidden in shadow, just beyond sight, facial features mostly obscured.

As he felt his way through the mist, staff extended before him, just for safety, Jannus felt his anxiety rising. He had to admit, he was afraid of the coming confrontation. What would happen? What would he say, or do, when they finally came face to face? Jannus had wondered more than once, why he did not just turn around. Go back home, and forget about all of this. Part of him wanted to make this choice; go back home, maybe open another bottle from the treasury, and just forget. He knew he could do it. In fact, he had become quite proficient at that. Forgetting. Sure, he could do so again, easily.

As he was walking slowly through the mist, Jannus tried to visualise the buildings he thought he might he passing. Most of the images he could conjure were from childhood, or at the very latest, his teenage years. He thought he might he walking past the old pub, "The Griffon". Jannus knew the dive was closed for many years now, but maybe the building was still there, now in the property of someone else, with a different purpose... Maybe the signature sign was still out front (gold on black), or perhaps it had been put away for good. *A place of unfulfilled dreams; sounds of the accordion during the refrain, misery loves company.*

Jannus remembered a particular girl in a yellow summer dress walking out of there, and an angry man being kept outside, a burden on his back, the girl with a hidden shadow in her chest. They had put capstones on top of the grave, Jannus seemed to recall. A third and last memory regarding The Griffon came to mind; three elderly folks (elderly to Jannus, at least) dancing in a circle under the sign, unmindful of any spectators, joyful in their later years.

Jannus recalled something that Mielle had said to him, during their walk through the woods. 'Human ambition is illimitable, Jannus, and so is their mendacity.' Her voice had been tinctured with the slightest sense of irony, yet he had believed the truth of her words. They had felt personal, somehow. 'Hope without deliverance, Jannus, is ever fatal. You may utter your defiance on the burning sands, yet that is the truth.'

Jannus had not argued with her, though he had doubted her words. They had seemed too personal, in a way, as though she had been trying to convince herself, rather than him. The collie had reacted differently, though. He had started to howl, and halfway through, the sound had changed almost to a glissando. Jannus had never heard that kind of howling. The collie had been silent after that, looking between himself and Mielle. Jannus had been worried something was wrong with the dog, but shortly after that, the collie had started panting again. He did not know why he should remember that just now.

Reminiscing brought about other childhood memories: the red swing with the broken rope, him hitting the ground, feeling the pain, but starting to laugh instead. When he had dug up potatoes with his bare hands; in turn, being yelled at from the dirt under the fingernails; later, alone in his room, crying, not understanding what he had done wrong. *When did I lose that ability?* Jannus wondered. The ability to create fantasy out of nothing with the innocence of a dreamer; joy in its simplest form.

As he felt the mist slowly lifting, Jannus could see clearly that he was close to the town proper now. He felt a short moment of relief that he had not been lost in the mist. And then, he realised that he was getting closer to his goal. As anxiety was rising, he once again lamented the absence of his medication. But then again, he had managed so far without it, had he not?

He recalled one of his former clients, a young woman in her early twenties, with her own form of anxiety. She had spoken of her childhood in great depth, as if she had been locked forever in that time. Not as a romanticised thing, though, oh no.

'It's as if I am inside the house, and everybody else is outside. My mum, my dad, my brothers, everybody. And I am always inside, looking out. It's all I remember. Is that normal?'

Jannus could not recall what he had told her, exactly. Maybe he had said something along the lines of 'Well, that it very understandable.' He could also have spoken of needs and desires and wishes unfulfilled. Of attachment, and of a child searching for safety, and meaning in its surroundings. Whatever he had told her then, he now hoped it had been helpful, or at least sufficient, in terms of the young woman accepting how those experiences had shaped her current life. What a sad part she had had to play.

As the mist had started to lift, like ashes on the

wind, Jannus had begun to use the staff more like a walking-supplement, for support. He could feel fatigue setting in, and he had no more supplies, having giving most of them to Johan of the Outer Isles. Fortunately, he was almost at his destination; no matter the development his home town had been through, he was most certain that a few shopkeepers would still make their trade here.

Jannus looked up. The mist had lifted, the last few ashes now completely scattered to the winds, and he was home. The daystar had reached its zenith; Jannus judged it to be about midday. The sun looked pale though, as if the mist still held some kind of unseen sway. Looking around, it did appear as if all the purple-black shadows were gone for good. *That must mean I am truly back in my own time and place, then?* Jannus had to admit to himself that he was unsure of this fact, at this point. And surprised at himself that he was not as freaked out by it as much as he would have imagined. *Guess you can get used to anything, then,* he thought, as he raised the staff to rest it upon his shoulder.

Am I truly home?

Home is truly a place of bitterness, and regret, Mielle thought, as she looked at the mist. She had told Jannus that the way forward was barred to her, yet that had been untrue. She remembered this place, all too clearly. She remembered the early beginnings, when all had been hopeful, and prosperous. Before the shadows had descended upon them all.

Choices had been made then — good and bad. Some even fatal, some of her own making. She had dealt her hand as best she could, and all had paid the price; herself most of all. What a lofty perch she had once maintained, even gripped, all too tightly. What would have happened if she had acted sooner? And with more compassion? Or less?

It was too late for her world, Mielle knew. Yet maybe she could still help Jannus, and his home. And hers; in truth, she had recognised the place almost immediately. The forest of Ir-Nos-Lia (though much smaller now), the High Hills, defenders of the land, and the Great Sea, still full of promises, back then. The town itself was much changed though. She had not cared much for the look of it, in truth. She had kept her silence to not disturb Jannus, though. This was his home, after all, and thus, close to his heart.

Much of who she had been still remained in her, and so she still felt certain obligations when she held people's hearts in her hands, even when she had made them hurt, and bleed, and break. Mielle would do all in her power to make sure she did not bestow this fate upon Jannus.

As she walked back to Ir-Nos-Lia and the power she hoped still remained there, she looked down at the beast following her footsteps. Was her own redemption almost at hand?

PART III

HOMELANDS

CHAPTER XVIII

Lost Friends of Mine

Jannus had never meant to visit the town cemetery. The former therapist had been here only twice before; once, during the occasion of his mother's funeral. His grandmother had stood by his side for unnecessary comfort.

The *second* time, he had come here alone to visit his grandmother's grave. *That* time he had very much needed some form of comfort, yet had found none.

His hometown's cemetery was not the sort you would find in the usual horror-flick; a most evil place of mist and shadows where the dead would await. No, this was a place of great comfort, well-kept by professional staff, that made sure everything looked proper, both for the people laid to rest there, and for those who came to visit. This place looked mostly peaceful and serene. The back-end of the cemetery was pretty close to the shore-line, though, Jannus noticed. In another decade or so, the whole thing might be submerged and consumed by the sea.

Only the front-gate lived up to a horrific potential. The gate screamed and groaned when he opened it.

Jannus looked around in embarrassment, but the cemetery appeared to have no visitors at this particular hour. Besides, the cemetery was situated near the edge of town. No one would care. The state of the cemetery gate seemed to have been deteriorating for a long while, so the locals were most likely accustomed to the sound. If they even cared at all.

His grandmother had sometimes joked around with her own passing. 'Somebody asked me what I would want when I died, Jannus,' she had said to him once, with an incredulous look. 'You know what I said to them, Jannus?' Jannus had not. 'Well, I said I most likely wouldn't care since I was dead and everything.' And then she had cackled. Jannus, not fully understanding, had only smiled, and chuckled politely.

As he was now walking down the gravelled paths between the rows of graves, Jannus thought he understood much better now; it was the living, the survivors, the ones that remained, who needed the help the most; the comfort. The dead were most likely all right, wherever they went to, if they went anywhere at all.

Jannus did not look too closely at the graves he was passing; he knew the two places where he wanted to go. It was not as if he missed everything, though; he was walking at a relatively slow pace, out of respect. Jannus had never been the most religious sort of person, yet he still adhered to certain principles, one of which had to do with letting people rest in peace. He passed graves with smaller headstones that signified a very young child had been laid to rest here. Jannus looked quickly away from those; he noticed three or four of them, and one would already have been too many, in his eyes.

And then he came upon a name which he had not expected, yet recognised immediately. The name of an old friend, almost forgotten. Jannus stopped at the grave, and knelt down to look closer at the name.

'Ah, Ben,' he said softly, almost reaching out with a hand. The grave seemed fairly well-kept; the headstone was one of the smaller ones, yet it was nicely placed amidst some greenery, which partly covered the stone. *Half in shadow, half in light,* he thought, as he knelt down.

Ben had been one of his closest friends, when they were both kids. Their backgrounds had been almost diametrically opposed; Jannus made his home on the northern high hill, above the rest of town. Ben, meanwhile, grew up in the Lower Ward, in some social-apartment complex. One of those buildings that had been originally meant for the modern family with modern needs. The reality had been quite different, as almost all of them ended up being classified as ghetto-areas, wherever they had been built.

They had a lot of things in common, though; their love of fantasy and science-fiction, games and books, and nature and sports. These were often combined; the local woods had proven quite the staging-ground for epic fantasy battles that they had either read about, or played. They had experimented with all sorts of different characterisations, different faces, and different looks.

Jannus looked closer at the dates on the grave. Ben had been one year younger than him, even though he in some regards had seemed older. More mature in some respects. It looked as though he had died eight years ago. Which meant that he had just made it to a few years beyond thirty. Of course, the gravestone made no mention of the cause of death, so no explanation there.

Yet, Jannus wondered, was it an accident? Terminal illness? Not natural causes, surely? Addiction, maybe? *I'm probably just projecting there,* Jannus thought, as he rose to a standing position again. Reminiscing, he reflected that he had actually never had a friend like Ben. There had never been any conflict between them, nor any sort of fallout. They had just drifted apart, as friends sometimes do.

A few porcelain vases were placed on Ben's grave. Each held a few flowers; one with white roses, the other one with tulips, one red, one yellow. *At least someone still looks out for you.* Jannus felt a sense of embarrassment and guilt, seeing these gifts for the deceased and beloved.

Moving on, his next destination was clear. Unlike his friend's grave, this one was not as well-visited. Well-kept, sure, since this was mostly done by personnel. Yet there were no flowers here; no one had left a personal or *familial* touch in a long while, it seemed. His mother's grave seemed mostly anonymous, compared to the majority here, apart from the "Unwitnessed" section of the cemetery.

Jannus had only been to see his mother's grave at her funeral. And never since. And his sister had not even attended *that*. And he would have been surprised if she had visited later. True enough, his sister had been "sent away", at the time of the funeral, so she did have an acceptable excuse.

Jannus did not have a lot of memories of his mother, that dark lady, who almost always had worn black, not out of preference or style, but out of necessity. Long sleeves and turtle necks. Sometimes her eyes had been darkened, too, by some "unfortunate event" (as they had been explained to Jannus, back then), and then they, too, had needed some sort of coverage. Jannus had never borne her any great affection; she had not been able to give him that much, anyway, so it had been most difficult to reciprocate. Yet now, as he stood here by her grave (Jannus was vaguely aware that he had not knelt down, this time), he found that he was beginning to see her in a somewhat different light.

His mother's main strength had been her silence, he thought. She had probably been navigating through some very difficult terrain (emotionally, relationally, cognitively), and though she had not always succeeded at this, Jannus thought that she had at least tried to maintain whatever composure she could. Not that

Jannus could find it within himself to actually *thank* her for this (*yet*), but he could at least appreciate her efforts.

He turned away from his mother's grave to his last destination. Down the gravelled path he went, passing even more broken dreams. He quickly found his grandmother's grave. For this one, Jannus chose to sit down on the gravel before the stone-marker with her name on it, legs folded as if in mindful meditation. She had been buried with her late husband, Jannus' grandfather, whom he had never known. 'A light in my dark, he was, Jannus,' his grandmother had once told him. Towards the end of her life, she had spoken of her late husband more and more. Even then, Jannus had understood that his grandmother missed him and somewhat secretly wanted to see him again. *Be* with him.

'You were also a light in *my* dark,' Jannus said softly, as he sat by her grave, legs folded as if he was but a boy, yet again. She had been his guidance, his leading star, to show him a way forward, and lent him a hand whenever he stumbled and fell. And he had always managed to rise up again. *Yet I might not have done so, again and again, if not for her,* Jannus mused, as he gently touched the stone-marker with his fingers.

Jannus had always seen her in the brightest of shades. Yet now, as he sat by her grave and looked at her name on the stone-marker, he wondered if she had not borne her own shadows in life, hidden deep, perhaps, to give aid to the boy who often came to her for comfort. How much of her own pain and grief and torment did she have to hide away from the light? Jannus did not like thinking of her this way, yet he felt it was important to consider. Did his grandmother have any regrets towards the end? About her own life? Or about the boy she had tried to help? Before her passing, Jannus had begun to diverge from the path she had directed him on. He had begun to stumble and fall, again. And that *last* time, she had not lent him a hand, for some reason…

His grandmother's grave was well-kept, with almost-fresh flowers nearly covering the ground next to the stone-markers. At first this confused Jannus, since he knew he himself had not paid a single visit since then (at this, he felt a painful sensation in his chest), and he almost knew, with certainty, that his sister had not either. She had never had the same bond with their grandmother as Jannus had. But then he remembered that his father had several (all estranged) siblings, most likely with their own offspring, who must have kept a maintenance toward *their* grandmother's grave.

Jannus felt a few tears fall from his eyes down onto the back of his hands, resting in his lap. Returning home had so far proved to be an emotional and reflective experience. Not that he regretted it; not at all. In fact, he had by now become convinced that this journey he was undertaking was most essential. Towards *what* exactly, he was still unsure. A change of some sort, certainly.

Jannus just wished he was more certain of his final destination, and whatever end game would await him. The envelope with the letter inside was still firmly placed in his front pocket. He made sure it was still there. There was a confrontation coming, and though he still dreaded the outcome, part of him also felt a certain sense of excitement. Another part of him just wanted *an end*.

Walking back towards the exit, he barely noticed a grave standing just a bit apart from the rest. It was of a grand design on a place where the ground was raised a couple of feet. Whoever the grave belonged to, it looked like that person had been buried with a nice view of everything; Jannus felt no inclination to pay a visit to that one, as he had decided not to gaze in that particular direction again.

He was oblivious to the gate's screaming as he left the cemetery.

Mielle was trudging her way back over the hill-top from whence they had come. Her thoughts turned to the past, wherein she had walked a similar path; she had once walked through yellow-brown grass, the fourth in line behind three men moving through the dark, making their escape.

They had fled from the great weapons of war, clever artifices of iron and fire, from which they had failed to protect themselves. Mielle shook her head in irritation as she increased her pace. She did not enjoy thinking of her own homelands, even as she had just guided Jannus to his. For her, it had become associated with undying memories in a prison of flame.

The opposing forces had given her a moniker, 'Dark Lady's Servant', which she had learned to bear as a badge of pride. Scorn and shame and blood and grief had clung to her like burned clothing, yet she would not falter. She felt something sting at her face, and she glanced up at the sky. Almost right above her, the daystar burned bright. "Highstar" they had called it, when their star had reached that point in the heavens above them.

Yet this one seemed a different star from the one she had known; this one burned brightly, oh yes. Yet for Mielle it seemed of a different hue; not yellow and red, but dark and blue and burning. Merciless, as it gazed down upon her, the heat almost too much to bear, cold in its disregard.

'Maybe this is my penance,' she mused, as she was nearing the forested hilltop. At her side, the beast continued to follow her. She was still unsure why it had chosen to do so; she had not made any effort to force the beast any particular way; not in the same manner she had guided Jannus to his destination.

At that thought, Mielle felt a stab of regret course through her. She bore Jannus no ill will of any sort; he seemed a decent man, yet bereft of soul's guidance and the shadows that followed in his wake. But it was too late for such misgivings. She had to do whatever was required of her, to restore the balance, to change back all those things that happened that were never meant to happen.

And that, as always, required some sort of sacrifice. She would do what she could for Jannus, of course. Yet she knew, almost with certainty, that it would not be enough. In her position she could nay afford friends or close relations of any sort. Allies, for a certainty, but nothing more.

She looked down again at the dog, who had remained at her side. 'If such a noble beast chooses to walk with me, maybe there is still hope for me, too,' she mused, as she entered the ancient forest of her own time, yet again.

CHAPTER XIX

Tears of My Father

Jannus had given up using the staff as a walking supplement; he had started to feel somewhat silly walking with it. First of all, it was unnecessary, and secondly, he had a rather vivid sensation that people were looking at him, wonderingly, from afar, because of it. The former therapist was well aware of the illogical nature of the thought, yet it remained strong enough to be directive. Instead, he had strapped it to his back in such a way that the backpack was somewhat holding it in place. The thing kept sliding though, from a position where the top of it stuck above his left shoulder, down to his waist. From time to time, he would readjust it, feeling silly all over again.

Jannus had decided to make a break westward before reaching the city centre, which, among other things, contained the town square, the heart of the town. If he had continued straight ahead, he would have continued uphill, right up to his family home.

But Jannus had reached a decision. Now that he was finally returning home, there were quite a few things he would like to be done with; things that were long overdue. After all, he was not sure he would ever return, one way or the other. Before he turned west along Hart Road, which led into the Industry Ward of his home town, he had another look at his childhood home, the mansion on the hill.

From here it looked different. Somehow, it looked less pristine, and more decrepit, in a way. As though it had lost its former glory, and was now desperately holding on to whatever it had left. It was still standing proud and tall above everything else in town, yet more alone and isolated. The sight of it was disturbing to Jannus: on the one hand, his childhood home had been the centre of his fears, the origin of whatever suffering he would live through later in life. Not the house itself, naturally, but all the things that had happened in it, all the things that had been missing. On the other hand, he felt excitement stirring as his end goal was almost within reach.

Walking onto Hart Road (named after a mayor before his time), Jannus found himself looked upward. Industry Ward had always been characterised by a great many buildings, most of them tall and grey. A generation ago, most of them had been factories. Later on they were replaced by an assortment of businesses; IT-security, insurance, a game-developing company, a great shopping mall with its own selection of different stores, a phone company, and many more. It seemed as if his home town was not as much of a "sleeping-town" as he had imagined.

Jannus was not that interested in all of these new business ventures, though. As Hart Road took a slight right turn, he found himself looking expectantly for something else, but his expectancy turned quickly to disappointment. He had imagined a great, tall building of black glass, where his father had worked. It had towered over everything back then, Jannus remembered, being the only building of its kind. Only the family mansion had stood higher, on its northern hill. Now, there was only an empty ground full of rubble. A work-site was developing next to it. Apparently, there were plans to make something else here. As Jannus got closer, he found the answer to what.

M.T. Constructions were building condominiums here, apparently. Under the construction company's name, on a sign outside the work-site, there was a slogan: "Safely & Efficiently -We Build for the Modern Family", they promised. Jannus took out the envelope from his pocket, and reached for the letter within. He quickly found the address written there and looked up at various signs surrounding the building site, for confirmation. As he finally found what he was looking for, Jannus found his whole body shudder. *Well, there it is, then.*

The address in the letter matched the one that had once housed his father's workplace, his *empire.* Jannus had never been inside the building when it had been standing tall: it had not been allowed. It had been a forbidden land, where his father had reigned. Or at least, so Jannus had believed, back then. His father had spoken much of his work-life at home; of the latest deal he had made, of all his successes, and none of his failures. After his father's death, Jannus had learned the more realistic version of the story. There was a selection of articles that came out, locally, and even nationally, a few months after his father's passing. The truth of it all was that the company had been near bankruptcy, and several lawsuits were underway. *"Legacy of Mr Rubens Destroyed"* and *"Fall of the House of Rubens"* were some of the headlines, Jannus still remembered, along with a picture of his father (very overweight in his later years, always with a stressed expression), and of their mansion home.

Jannus had not lived at home at that point, so he had not felt personally affected at the time (beyond feeling a certain measure of *schadenfreude*). And he had suspected that quite of the few of the locals had felt that way, too. His father had not been a popular man, by any means; someone you had been friendly to in person, certainly, but also a man who had been talked about behind his back. But as he now looked at the rubble of the proud, black glass tower, where his father had once ruled from the top floor, Jannus felt a different sort of feeling emerge.

He wondered why he had buried the memory of this place so deep that it had taken him several days to recognise it. And even more worrisome, had the sender of the letter known? His father *had* been somewhat known in the parts, being a local celebrity of sorts. And would it then be totally implausible that *someone* would be able to make the association to Jannus himself? *I guess not,* Jannus thought, putting the envelope back again, still worried. The *why* of it still eluded him. Why bring him here to this place that was no more… that held no meaning, any more? And then he looked up at his childhood home still high above. *My true destination.*

Seeing his home this relatively brought about thoughts of his late mother. She had always been great at hiding herself, to make herself unnoticeable. She had been great at navigating through all sorts of social circles without coming under anyone's serious regard. Jannus had not known a lot of his mother's childhood life, and he had never met his grandparents on that side of the family. They had been estranged from their daughter for as long as Jannus could remember, and he had never asked his mother (or father) why.

Whatever the cause(s), his mother had become quite proficient at hiding, and she had transferred this ability to her son. Not necessarily in a conscious way, but Jannus could see now he had learned to mimic that particular trait of hers quite well; maybe even better.

Jannus began to notice that more and more people were now beginning to emerge onto the streets; people going on their way to work, and even a couple of kids on their bikes passed by. No one seemed to notice Jannus there, and he did not recognise any one. He turned back to the empty grounds in front of him.

From his grandmother's influence, he had tried to do everything with a great heart, and in this, Jannus felt he had only partly succeeded. These last couple of years had been quite empty of heart, he had to admit to himself, but before that, he had at least always tried to emulate his paternal grandmother in this. And from his father…

Jannus continued on his way. Hart Road kept turning right until it led all the way to the docks district, which was another place he wanted to visit. More and more people passed by, and the morning traffic had begun to escalate. Though he was loathe to admit it, Jannus knew that he had inherited a certain need for recognition from his late father. Not that there was something innately wrong with wanting to be recognised. But when it was flavoured with a certain arrogance when you got it, and a peculiar decrease in self-worth when you did not, there was something you could be concerned about. Jannus knew very well it was also a matter of degrees; almost everyone wanted to be recognised in some manner, to be sure. It was the extremes you had to look out for. If you could not function at all, if it became an obsession, *then* you had to be careful.

For his father it had certainly become so, even to the detriment of his health, and his family life. Both. Another thing he shared with his father was his temperament, only it was expressed in different ways. His father's rage had been directed outward, towards whoever was near — usually his mother, or Jannus himself. *And probably also his employees,* Jannus thought to himself, as an elderly man walking with a cane smiled and nodded at him, as they passed each other on the sidewalk. Jannus found himself smiling and nodding back, not out of immediate recognition, but politeness. *That* came from his grandmother, he knew. The elderly man most likely came from the docks district that Jannus himself was heading towards.

His own temperament was directed more inwardly, Jannus reflected — towards the self. His rage often became mired in self-blame and general negative and derogatory thinking. Whenever things did not go his way, he would usually blame himself first. Oh, he would blame other people too, certainly. But the main thing that would always return was why he himself had failed yet again.

All of this made Jannus feel a slight empathy towards his late father; sympathy, not so much. In most ways he still regarded his father the same way. Yet now he recognised that a bigger part of him may have originated from his father. And not *all* of it had been bad.

Jannus noticed a sign on the other side of the street: Euphoria's Rest. It seemed like a hostel. *Another new edition to my home town?* He waited at the curb to get a chance to cross, yet traffic appeared to be increasing in this part of town, at this time of day. Jannus suddenly remembered that he once saw his father cry. Only the once. Yet it had been very revealing.

His father had been in his cups at the time, lying on the couch in one of the living rooms. Jannus had heard somebody cry, and with a child's curiosity, he had left his own room and explored the mansion until he found his father in another part of the building. Mr Rubens (the elder) had been facing inward, so Jannus had not been able to see his father's face. He could only see the body convulse, and hear the sounds of crying. And then, ever so softly, he had heard his father's voice, yet with a much lighter tone, almost like a child's.

'Please stop hitting me, stop hitting me, won't you stop? Will someone help? Please help?"

Little Jannus had not understood what his father had been talking about at the time, nor what he had been crying about. But he *did* understand that he would not want his father to notice him there.

Jannus finally found a moment to cross the road... Or *thought* he did, anyway, as some driver honked his horn behind him, in three, short, sharp bursts. He waved a hand lazily behind him, as a way of a non-apology, and the unknown driver honked a final time; in appreciation or acceptance, Jannus did not care to find out.

Jannus recalled that his father always got tools for his birthday. Jannus' mum always bought his father tools for his birthday. Even as a kid, Jannus had begun to wonder; he never saw his father utilise any of them. Whenever there was anything practical that had to be done around the house, his father always got outside help, and called for professional help.

'I haven't the time, my dear,' Jannus once overheard his father saying to his mother. Whenever he had heard the words "my dear", Jannus had his anxiety trigger. 'You know I would do it myself, otherwise.' His father's voice would brook no argument.

Much later, Jannus would come to suspect that his father actually did not know how to use all the tool-gifts he had received. And maybe, just maybe, it had been a sort of silent revolt on account of his mother. It would have been just like her.

A broken man with a broken leg, trying to find a new way through his world, Jannus now thought of his father. *A modern man trying to retain his soul?*

From the outside looking in, the hostel did not look too impressive, and as he entered, his suspicions were confirmed. Everything was as one would expect. Dried-out plants in the hallway, the floor only half-cleaned, and a thin layer of dust seemed to cover almost everything. It looked like the cheapest place in town for busy and poor travellers, with modest needs for accommodation. A young person sat behind a counter. Jannus judged him to be in his early twenties, maybe late teens. So far, he had not reacted to Jannus entering the premises, and small wonder. A set of headphones sat upon his unkempt, pale hair and Jannus could faintly hear the sounds of some hard-rock band, almost recognisable to his ears.

Finally, the young man looked up. To Jannus, his eyes looked dull, and uninterested. Yet his smile was brilliant and welcoming, to Jannus' great surprise.

'Pleasant greetings, sir,' the young man began, in a voice more cultivated than Jannus had expected. 'Do you want a room? Private? Or shared?'

'The former, please, if you have it,' Jannus responded. It had been over twenty years since he had stayed at a hostel, and he had no desire to stay at this one any more than necessary. But he felt it wise to check in *somewhere,* while here, and he had only brought a limited amount of funds along. So, a hostel it would be.

'That's great sir, I think we have one at the ready.' The young man turned to his computer, probably to confirm his statement. Gazing behind the counter, Jannus saw a small coffee table, and a three-legged chair that the young man in front must have been sitting on. On the table was a thick, hardcover book, over a thousand pages, at least. Tilting his head, Janus saw the name of the author, *James Joyce,* and underneath, four titles printed too small for Jannus to see from the other side of the counter.

Jannus found himself reassessing the young man in front of him. *Ever so quick to judge, eh Janus?* he thought, in a self-recriminatory manner.

'Ah yes, I thought so,' the young man said, ever smiling. 'A private room, as you requested. For how many nights, sir?'

'Just two, please. Yes, that should do it. Payment

upfront, naturally?' he asked.

The young man nodded, took the money and made the reservation. Handing Jannus the key, he smiled at him, and returned to the three-legged chair, and his book. *His eyes did not look dull,* Jannus realised, finding his way to his appointed room. *They looked tired. From all the heavy-reading, probably.*

The room in question was nothing to write home about; a single bed with a thin mattress, a dormitory-style of sleeping arrangement. The room smelled stale underneath an odorous veneer of cleaning products. Other than the bed, the only other furnishings were a chair, and a table. On the latter was placed a welcome greeting, and a folder of practical information.

The dark blue carpet was marred by burn-marks, left from cigarettes, most likely, despite the 'No-smoking' sign on the door. And there were several pictures, or paintings, rather, on the wall. A painting of an island, partly covered in mist. Another painting was of a lighthouse, shining below a darkened sky. And a third one, beside a mirror, depicting sea and sky, and a fisherman occupying a small boat in the centre.

On the way to his room, Jannus had passed a door to a shared bathroom, and a sign pointing the way to a communal kitchen. He had no immediate wish to make use of either. He *was* feeling tired though, and decided to lie down on the bed; not to sleep, only to rest.

He took off his backpack, and rested the staff on the wall beside the door. As he lay down, hands folded behind his neck, Jannus closed his eyes.

He found himself thinking of Mielle. And of what he thought he had already learned from her. Almost from the very beginning, from the first dreamscape where he had made her acquaintance, he had admired the way she had seemed to hold herself, with a certain grace and *nobility*. Not that he thought himself noble in any way, but there was something about her that Jannus found himself wanting to emulate. Rather than walking blithely through the world, as had been his usual wont for many years, maybe he could approach things a bit more reflectively. Wisely. And yes, maybe even just a bit more *nobly*. Part of him thought he was mentally unstable for wanting to mimic someone whom he was not even sure was *real*. And another part of him wanted to *thank* her, whenever they would meet again, whether it proved to be in this world, or the dreamscape.

And oh, how he could just imagine all the celebrants gathered together. Not in celebration of his success, oh no... It was too long ago that the gentleman of leisure could have believed that! He had been a dreamer once, and he had paid for that, again and again. He had been walking around the edge of the room he had been in for so long, from corner to corner. As if looking for an exit, and failing. The chair in the middle of the room he had been sitting in a long, long time, was gone. The gentleman was unable to remember if he had put it away himself, or if someone had come by to collect it.

Somehow, he doubted either scenario.

In its place was a pile of skins — seal from the look of it, though the gentleman was no expert in maritime affairs. They were silver and bluish-grey, with black-spotted markings. Some kind of strange fungus seemed to be growing on them, a white fungal coating on most of the skin-surface he could see, without touching them. Similar to the experience with the missing chair, the gentleman was unaware if he himself had procured the skins, or if somebody else had left them there. But because of the nature of the skins themselves, and their fungal growth, he was becoming more and more desperate for an exit. Every turn of the room came faster and faster, and yet he found no exit. He seemed to remember that the room used to have a door. Or a window, maybe, with frightful light coming in seeking to harm him. Did he misremember? Though there were now no windows nor door, the room was somehow sufficiently lit that he could see where he was going, and he also had a clear view of the skins in the middle of the room. Despite his rising desperation, he still had faith that this would soon end, and all would get what they deserved. Someone would soon come to this room, and then it would all be over. Finally.

CHAPTER XX

Fear of the Veil

After having fallen asleep, Jannus had woken in his hostel room, confused and groggy, with an aching back. Hurriedly, he put on his backpack, secured the staff on his back, and had left his room. He had gathered from the clock in the hallway, that he had, at most, lost a couple of hours. Outside, it looked like late afternoon. Leaving the hostel, he did not look to see if the young man was still behind the counter. And absently, Jannus wondered why the young man had never approached him about the staff on his back. He made his way to the docks district.

As a child, this particular area had been another sort of playground for him. Not in a practical sense, like the forest on the southern hill. But more in his mind's eye; looking out at the sea, which had seemed to stretch on forever in his boy's view of the world, he had imagined countless adventures. He had even imagined (and half-way planned) a way for him to sneak onto a boat, or maybe one of those great tourist ships that would sometimes lie at anchor, just a mile or so from the coastline. The harbour had not been large enough for the grander ships, so Jannus had only been able to gaze at them from a distance, which had propagated his fantasies of a possible life at sea. Ironically enough, he had travelled quite a lot as an adult, mostly with his former wife, since she had loved to travel. But they had never journeyed by sea.

Walking steadily and looking about, curiously, the docks district was another source of disappointment for Jannus. As he had been approaching the district, he had heard all the familiar sounds; waves crashing against the pier, the cries of the seagulls, and different kinds of machinery being operated. A whole host of memories had resurfaced in his mind along with the auditory stimuli. But rather than the tilted romantic view he had of it as a child, he now saw it through a more realistic lens. Yes, the grand sea was there as it (almost) always had been, stretching out before him, apparently endlessly, filling out the whole horizon. Yet now, as an adult, he knew, of course, the falseness of that promise. You could not see any other land on the horizon, true enough, but forty or fifty miles northwest of here, Jannus knew you would the country's largest isle: Bright Haven. The origin of that name eluded Jannus, but he knew that the first thing you would notice approaching the isle from the sea was a grand old lighthouse, guiding the seafarers on their way.

He could not see Bright Haven from the docks though, only the horizon with its fickle promises. Jannus walked by the old toll building, now appropriated as a museum of sorts, judging by the signs and posters out front. The only thing left from the old days, on that great red-bricked building, was a huge steel anchor above the double-doorway, with the city emblem in the centre. Jannus had planned that he would walk along the docks all the way to where the path led back northeast toward the city centre. There were still a few visits he had to make before ascending the hill to his childhood home.

Next, he passed 'The Lookout', the dive at the docks. Jannus had never been but remembered all the stories that he had *heard* being told in there; most of the talk inside was said to be mostly about the concerns of the day, to which *everybody* at the bar was reported to have the correct answers and solutions. He and Ben had also heard that people inside had whispered secret legends of Bright Haven, and of all the mysterious things that were sure to be happening there.

Walking by, Jannus felt a slight urge to step inside, just for a snifter or two, to fortify himself for what he assumed to be the last lap of his journey. Yet, this time, he recognised the sensation for what it was, and kept going. Besides, there were most likely people inside, who he *still* wanted to avoid, mostly.

Before he reached the end of the docks, Jannus passed by another familiar sight; a lot of places had changed their names or signs over the years, he had already noticed. Yet, the Merchant Guild still bore its name, and its old sigil; the name written in black on gold, over a circular frame depicting a boat on water, heading towards a light house. *Maybe towards a Bright Haven?* Jannus mused, as he left the Guild behind.

Eleanor Way led (the way) back to the city centre from the north side of the docks. If Jannus recalled his history correctly, he surmised Eleanor had been the wife of the old mayor, Hart. He had never paid much attention to local history when he lived here, but now Jannus found himself rather curious.

Hart and Eleanor, Eleanor and Hart. Jannus got the sense that something important was hidden in those names. Something important to him, perhaps? Eleanor Way was a two-way street about a mile long, connecting the docks to the city centre. Along the way, Jannus passed a well-to-do residential area, which was now a part of what was once known as the Upper Ward district.

A lot of familiar sights met him here; this was where his grandmother (and grandfather, before Jannus' time) had lived almost their whole lives. Judging by the people he saw in the streets, most people here were elderly. Yet the sight of a few playgrounds between the houses made Jannus surmise that a few families with children also made their home here. And sure enough, just a few seconds later, a couple of kids, two boys, passed him by on bikes, surprising him from behind. Jannus was mostly surprised that he had not noticed them beforehand; they were yelling and laughing, and they kept passing each other on their bikes, as if in playful competition. The sight made Jannus smile.

Jannus felt a sudden hunger; he had not had anything to eat since yesterday, if he recalled correctly. He partly regretted giving most of his supplies to Johan of the Outer Isles. But then again, the old man had seemed grateful for the gesture. He knew that the town square would offer quite a few selections of food and drink. And before he reached the square, Jannus would pass by a supermarket or two, if they were still there. He had not regretted not utilising the communal kitchen at the hostel, despite his growing hunger.

Before that, he had one more important destination in mind; probably the most important one, other than the mansion itself: his grandmother's house, where his heart had found a home. It was situated at the edge of the residential area, probably the smallest house in the vicinity. Standing before it, Jannus felt relaxed. As a child, the walls had been painted white, door and window red; it had been repainted in the intervening years: Aegean-blue walls, and the door and kitchen-window which were visible from the street, raven-black. The small, front garden seemed well kept, but his grandmother's old window-curtains were long gone, of course. They had been replaced with shades, household white. Part of him wanted to knock on the door, to get a view of the inside. But then again, he did not know what possible explanation he would give to the current owners that would be adequate.

Instead, he looked at the two neighbouring houses, both of similar size to his grandparents' home, though both with a section added on the western side. An old woman was outside the front of her house, opening her mailbox. *Maybe getting today's newspaper?* Jannus thought, as he nodded and smiled at her. The old woman did not change her neutral expression, and closed the door behind her. *Did she recognise me? Remember little boy Jannus as he came to visit her neighbour?* Jannus was unsure. Had the old woman turned his back on him as a coincidence? Had it been intentional? Jannus shook his head. Some of the old negative thoughts were re-emerging again, always delighted to frame everything in a darker light. He had become accustomed to restructuring such thinking; in fact, it was his very profession. Yet as always, there was a possibility that you yourself could succumb to the very things you warned others against.

And sure enough, as soon as those same old doubts made themselves known again, Jannus felt his anxiety rising, bubbling up from the pit of his stomach, tightening his chest, and constricting his throat. As always, the sensation almost became unreal, as if something *broke,* and he had lost part of himself, yet again. Almost in desperation, Jannus put his hand on the envelope in his front pocket, as if reassuring himself of the only thing that still made this fool's quest feel somehow *real.* Real enough to continue, at least.

Looking at his grandmother's old house again, he remembered what a haven it had once been for him. Jannus had never met his grandfather, but he suddenly recalled one of the few times his grandmother had spoken of him. She had found some old photographs in the cupboard, hidden away in a used cigar-box, silver and gold. The box had held quite a few old photos, one of which depicted a celebration of Saturnalia. One of the other photographs — black and white, and the one of most personal interest to Jannus - had been of his grandmother, and her siblings, all long gone. Jannus had never known his grandmother as a girl, naturally, but the girl in the photograph must have been about eight or nine. Three of her siblings had been younger, Jannus knew, and three older. She had been the middle child, with four brothers, and two sisters.

The photograph had once been broken in two in the middle, Jannus remembered, but someone had stitched it back together again. As his grandmother had been placed in the middle of her siblings when the photograph had been taken, she had suffered the most; the gash had been down the middle of her face. Jannus could recall how his grandmother had still held the photograph fondly.

She had spoken of her late husband then — Jannus' grandfather. 'Oh, he could tell stories, Jannus,' she had told him. 'From the times before he met me, of course. Your grandfather had travelled all over the world, little Jan. Almost, anyways! He talked about his travels in the Arctic, of all the things he had seen, fauna and flora both; of lime-grass and alpine fox-tail, even white arctic bell-heathers!'

Jannus had not known any of these names when he had heard them, yet it had triggered his imagination. He wished he had been there himself.

'Oh, Jannus... how he could talk to me of caribou and seals, and of mountain sorrels as he had ascended the heights all the way up there.' His grandmother had told him all of this with great excitement, but then her demeanour had changed, and the shift in mood had been palpable.

'Once, Jannus, your grandfather had suffered a terrible trichinosis infection on one of his expeditions. I won't bother you with the details, Jannus, but oh, how he had come close to passing the veil back then. "Passing the veil" had become his grandmother's way of explaining death to Jannus. The conversation with the photograph had taken place just a few years before her own passing, and Jannus suspected that she had become quite fearful, herself, at the end.

The memory of his grandmother speaking of his grandfather, and indirectly of her own passing, made Jannus reflect on one of his former clients. A woman in her mid-fifties had been afraid of sleeping alone in the dark. She had lost her lover of many years in the middle of the night. He had been having seizures, which had made her awake in the dark. Her lover had died that night, and the experience had been so traumatic for her that afterwards she had trouble sleeping alone, and in the dark, to the extent that she always had to have someone to be around her; usually friends or family.

'That must be somewhat difficult from a practical sense, is it not?' he had asked her, and she had confirmed. She always had to plan how to spend her night, so as not to sleep alone. That meant she had to rely on a lot of people around her, all the while feeling guilty for being so much trouble to those very people.

'Do you believe they think you are trouble to them?' he had asked her. She had not been able to verify that, naturally, but that was how she had felt and thought. Very much a spiritual woman, his client had started the sessions with the belief that her former lover might have been possessed. And what made her so afraid was the notion that she herself might be the next one in line to be possessed. That something was in there, *haunting* her.

With some difficulty he had tried to fit her particular beliefs in with some cognitive restructuring. '*If spirits can possess, might it be that they can also protect?*' he had offered her. 'I'm not a priest', Jannus had emphasized back then. 'But might it be there is someone there to guard you, not to *haunt* you?' That had made sense to his client, and after this, they had worked together, step by step, to figure out how she could get closer to her goal of finally being able to sleep alone at night, in the dark, by herself.

Before he left the residential area behind, Jannus saw another playground. A girl, aged about seven or eight, maybe, was seemingly playing alone; no other kids were visible, and the girl seemed without adult supervision, as well. Jannus tried not to rush to any sort of judgement, yet he had encountered a lot of kids in his former work-life; children alone and isolated, not being given the proper care by those who should have given it. The girl's clothes — jeans, and a white summer-shirt — seemed clean enough from his perspective. Her curly-blonde hair flowed freely about her shoulders. The playground contained swings, and a see-saw, rubber tyres for jumping on, and a sandbox of sorts, with short wooden blocks encircling the sand.

It was more so the girl's mannerisms or behaviour that had caught Jannus' attention, apart from her apparent loneliness. She was sitting on the sand between the swings and the see-saw. The girl had a yellow hand-shovel in one hand, which she used to fill up a bucket of similar colour. When she had filled the bucket with sand, she padded it down with the shovel to make an even surface, and then poured it all out again, repeating the process.

How long the girl would have repeated this, Jannus did not know, as she escaped his sight; the road had risen slightly, and then descended again, getting closer to the city centre. Ahead of him, he saw the signs of a few shops, one on this side of the street, and another one on the opposite side. Both had new names. "Brooks' Grocery Store" had become "Spencer's" in the intervening years, while "Upper Ward Market" was now "General Market". When Jannus got closer, he saw another, smaller sign beneath the "Market" sign. "Buy

Cheap, Buy Quality", it said. *The old Upper Ward would never have gone for that,* Jannus mused, as he went into Spencer's. The store, as a whole, seemed unremarkable; it looked like most grocery stores that he had ever frequented. Maybe they had the same designer? He remembered Brooks, the old owner; a gnarly old man with only a few strips of grey hair above the ears. He had been a kindly old man, though, always with a smile and a glint in his eye for the customers. Though Jannus had never invested himself much in local news after he had left his hometown, he had come across the news of the old man's retirement almost by chance. Brooks had been eighty-seven before he retired, and he had passed only a few years after that. Jannus bought himself a couple of sandwiches (one with egg and salmon, another one with ham and cheese), and some spring water.

Devouring both, he walked slowly towards the town square; Jannus could feel that something was imminent, something was approaching him. Just as he had taken a big gulp of spring water, Jannus felt a short, sharp pain in his head. He staggered and faltered, and raised a hand to his temple, as the pain made him bend forward. Jannus stood there for what seemed like a couple of minutes. Despite his state, he had the awareness that no one spoke to him, or reached out a helping hand.

When he stood back up, he felt a certain dizziness, and it took him a while to feel that the world around him had once again reasserted itself. Jannus looked up at the sky; it looked like several hours had just passed, with the daystar no longer high in the sky, but almost settled low in the western sky. Now everything looked purple-dark again, with few strips of orange-red slashing the sky here and there.

Having recovered himself, Jannus started walking again. He had finally reached the town square, the beating heart of his home.

'Welcome to Piazza Cavalcante," a familiar voice spoke behind him. "The High Court of Forinata."

CHAPTER XXI

Piazza Cavalcante

'A place of great regret, and sorrow.' Mielle came up behind him. Jannus was about to greet her pleasantly, but her countenance stopped him. More than ever before, Jannus thought that Mielle emanated a sort of strange, numinous quality.

Her outfit had also changed somewhat; over her usual robes, she wore a thick, scarlet cloak that dragged a foot or two behind her on the ground, and a currently raised hood. She walked ahead of him, into the centre of what he had known as the town square, and she had called "Piazza Cavalcante." Usually, Jannus knew, this place would be filled with people, old and young, singles and families, enjoying the mid-town bustle, sharing coffees and ice-creams, and all manner of confections, here at the city's beating heart.

Now, in its dreamscape version, it was empty. Almost. As he joined Mielle in the centre, Jannus began to see something; shades, or shadows, dark and light, moving about. Some of them stood together, as if in conversation, others appeared to be on their way to somewhere else, in their own time and place, since they left the plaza, and thereby, Jannus' vision of them.

'The High Court of who?' he asked.

'Forinata,' she simply said. Jannus knew Mielle well enough, at this point, not to ask again, but awaited her further explanation. And he *had* noticed that Mielle seemed to shiver at her mention of that particular name, as if she had just felt a cold wind hit them.

'This was once a place of joy, and celebration, Jannus,' she finally continued. She gave him a sharp look. 'And communion.' Jannus refrained from commenting that it still was; he got the sense that they most likely meant different things concerning the concepts of joy, celebration and communion.

'Even the Mountain Wanderers came to visit and pay their respects at our celebrations.' *Pay their respects to who?* Jannus wondered. Mielle started to walk slowly around Jannus in a circle. He got the odd feeling that he actually *was* present in some sort of ancient, or medieval court, standing trial.

'This was not a place of altercations, Jannus, or *conflict.* But for friendly debates and celebrations. The plaza would be surrounded by colourful spears, stabbed into the ground.' She kept walking around him while keeping eye contact. Jannus decided not to turn around with her, so she kept getting out of view, while walking behind him, still explaining, until she stepped into view again.

'Not as symbols of aggression, you understand, but of *community.* The spears were stuck into the ground, hafts facing outward. All covered brilliantly in starlight cloth to celebrate and show our thanks.'

Despite himself, Jannus could imagine it well enough; his own example of coffee and ice-cream and confections seemed rather dull compared to what she was telling him. Suddenly, one of the shades around them gained a bit in substance, and Jannus could clearly see a man, somewhat elderly in appearance (*roughly the same age as my father would have been,* he thought absently), stepping into view. Surprised, Jannus stepped backwards, while taking the staff from his back, holding it out in front of him, as if to protect himself.

'No fear,' Mielle said sharply. 'He is not here to harm; this ghostly resonance was but a penitent. He is here because his pain still holds him.'

Jannus took a closer look at the shade in front of him. The figure did not seem to recognise or acknowledge him in the slightest. The man walked with his own spear in hand (*maybe a hunter,* Jannus thought), with a fierce and somehow pained grin in his expression. And then he was gone again.

Mielle resumed her explanation. 'Until one day we were given a warning.' She stopped, and pointed at the ground, right at Jannus' feet. 'There, in the centre, was placed a story of bones.' Mielle became silent again, her eyes fixed on the ground. Jannus looked at her hand and saw it was actually shaking. *Is she reliving all this? Experiencing it all over again?* Jannus did not ask any of these questions, knowing he would probably not get an understandable answer, but he could not help *thinking* about them. That was one of the things he had learned to appreciate about Mielle; not matter her strange, regal ways, she did awake his curiosity.

When Mielle began talking again, it sounded as though she were reciting something: '*The head and three, uppermost, cervical vertebrae were mostly separated from the body proper; the head was held in place only by shreds of dried-out skin.*' Then she finally looked at him again. 'A warning given, Jannus. A warning not heeded.'

'A warning of what, my lady?' Jannus could not help himself asking.

Mielle smiled sadly at him. 'Of regret, dear Jannus. Of all the sorrow to come. The music plays and we are forced to dance to its whims.' Mielle knelt down, and gathered some dirt from the ground. Muttering under her breath, she threw some of it above her left shoulder, some in front of her, and the remaining part above her right shoulder, until her hand was empty again.

'Yet first came treachery, Jannus. Treachery always comes before the sorrow. "*One prepared always loses by delay,*" the wise councillor spoke, that false alchemist.' Jannus noticed the first hints of anger in Mielle's voice, at the mention of this councillor.

'Forinata?' he asked.

She nodded. 'Aye, Forinata, the First Inquisitor and Ruler of the High Court. Once known as a skilled alchemist, and a most wise councillor.' A brief flash of horror crossed her expression, before the anger returned, her cheeks gaining in colour. 'And oh, how he put those well-learned abilities to *great* use in his later vocation.'

Up until now, Jannus had had a rather romantic or rosy vision of what Mielle had told him, despite all the shades still moving about. He was excited by the tales that Mielle told him, and part of him wanted to be there, in that distant dream-past that she described. *Aye, the past is not always what we think it is; it is always flavoured with personal meaning and motivation. For myself, my childhood home has become a place of negativity, of something unwanted...* And yet the things Mielle spoke of, a far-past, or another place entirely, became almost romanticised in his mind. *The further away you are, eh?* he mused.

It all used to mean something. Or did it? Part of him wanted to leave his mortal remains behind and join this world Mielle spoke of. To be sure, all the stuff about inquisitors and penitents did not seem all that attractive, but compared to his own world, or specifically, his own daily life, all these things Mielle described seemed as if they had some sort of meaning and significance. *Quite unlike my life,* he thought.

Mired in his own web of thoughts, it took Jannus a while to realise that Mielle had resumed her story.

'We could not be corralled, not ever again. Yet when you try to scale the heavens against the gods, there are dire consequences and ramifications. We dared to be impertinent; we crossed the thresholds of the boundaries we were *given*. And we paid, Jannus. We paid, again and again.'

None of them spoke for a while after that. Even the shades seemed to have reduced their roaming about. 'Why are we here, Mielle?' Jannus finally asked.

She did not look at him, but somewhere beyond him. Where he could not fathom, since the whole square — or 'Plaza' — was enfolded in mist. 'This is the heart of things, Jannus. The Plaza, the beating heart of our community. It remains such a place, though it beats ever slower.'

Jannus nodded, since this was somewhat in alignment with his own observations; he well remembered the town square from his childhood and youth, and while it had definitely been full of life and love and laughter, he had always thought there was something missing. Lacking.

A beating heart losing its momentum, every beat not as forceful and sure of itself as the former. Jannus cocked his head, and half-expected to hear such a heartbeat, a *pulse,* getting slower and slower. Practically, he could not, naturally, but he could certainly imagine one.

'I see you understand, Jannus?'

'All too well, Mielle,' he said in answer. She had still not looked at him, but kept staring into the mist, as if in search of something. *Or as if she is waiting,* he thought. Jannus frowned. There had been something about Mielle since this latest appearance of hers; whether it was in her demeanour, or the way she had spoken of all these past events, he was unsure.

But something had made him just a bit suspicious of her. He suddenly came upon a decision. Jannus reached into his front pocket, and took out the letter, his own personal reason for coming all this way.

'I think I need to show you something, Mielle.' He held out the letter to her.

She did not reach for it, but kept her arms within the folds of her robes. 'What is it, Jannus?' Slightly embarrassed, he opened the envelope, and took out the four-page letter. 'A missive of sorts?' Mielle asked. 'A correspondence?'

Jannus was at first confused, but then nodded, finally understanding. 'Yeah, I suppose you could say that.' He quickly read through the pages. The content was as he recalled. Almost. He could not put his finger on it, but he thought a single word or two was changed. Or maybe rearranged? Was he misremembering? He had not been in the best state of mind when he had read it back home, to be sure. But Jannus was almost positive that somehow was slightly off, here.

'I got this letter, or *missive*, here, a while back. From someone I don't know, or maybe I do. Not positive about that.' Jannus kept shifting between the pages to see if he could catch more anomalies. 'I think it's from someone who wishes harm upon me, Mielle. Someone from my past, maybe. Somebody who thinks

I might have wronged them.' He looked at her. 'Somebody who wants payback for something they think I did to them.'

For a few moments, Mielle looked at him in silence. A shade seemed to bump into her, though she did not seem to notice it. Jannus got the strange sensation that most of the shades seemed to keep a healthy distance from her, whereas they kept flooding around him, not keeping a respectful distance.

'What was the nature of the damage you caused them, Jannus?' she asked, with a curious frown in her expression.

'Well, I don't rightly know, Mielle.' Her frown deepened. 'Well, I don't!' he said, exasperated. 'But I need to find out, Mielle. I *want* to find out. I need answers!' At that, she nodded and smiled at him, as if congratulating him on a wise decision.

'I think I understand your motivation, dear Jannus. And your possible peril.' Mielle stepped closer, her robes almost flowing behind her, hands still unseen amidst her attire. 'You seek to confront this personage, to gain knowledge of their animosity toward you?'

'Well, kind of — I guess,' he said, somewhat confused by her wording. Jannus hesitated, then continued. 'But I think something has changed now, Mielle. In the letter, I mean. Some of the words, they—' He shifted the pages again to find the exact words. 'Here... and *here.*' He pointed out the words with a finger. 'Those don't seem the same to me. Not quite.'

Jannus kept looking at the letter, and at Mielle, back and forth, back and forth. She *almost* had not changed her expression. But Jannus had been very observant of her while showing her the letter, and he noticed it; just a slight slip, an almost imperceptible shift of the eyes that gave him a suspicion that she *might* know something of the letter.

He was hesitant to ask it of her, though. Why, he did not know. After all, this was just a dreamscape, right? Sure, one of those he seemed to have *walked* into, while wide awake, rather than one of those he gained access to while sleeping. And that fact disturbed him. The 'sleeping ones' he could explain away easily. They might still just be dreams, however real they felt. But *these*? The ones he had experienced on this journey? Were they dreams? Or real? A symptom of something pathological? Jannus feared the answer to those questions.

'So, you question the content of the missive, Jannus?' Her regal tone had re-entered her voice, he noticed. She moved from her position to stand at his side, gazing at the letter in his hands. 'I do not recognise the symbols on the pages, Jannus.' She looked up at him. 'Are they in your language?'

Jannus looked at her in confusion. 'Well, yes, the same language we're using right now, Mielle. Right?' She looked at him, seemingly puzzled.

Is language different in the dreamscape? Jannus wondered. He thought not, since it sounded the same to his ears, and he could easily understand Mielle, though her phrasing sounded a bit archaic.

Mielle had given up reading the letter, it seemed, and she walked away, standing just outside the centre of the inner circle of the plaza. 'I have not dealt in missives for a long time, Jannus', she said, almost wistfully. 'Sometimes even words you think you write or speak for yourself are not truly your own… and the words that you think are your own often have a foreign nature to them, do they not?'

That was true enough, Jannus supposed.

In his work as a therapist, he had often worked with words and language. Or narratives, rather. How they were often infused with meaning and purpose, how to restructure them, to give it meaning and purpose where there had been none, or change them where the meaning and purpose had become negative, and self-undermining. And how easily it was to ascribe something we thought we had thought ourselves to someone else, and vice versa.

Holding the letter in his hand, he thought of his grandmother. They had become pen-pals in the last few years of her life. She had never been a strong writer, but her writing had worsened in each letter; her style had never been pretty, but the worse she got health-wise, the worse her letters became, in terms of order, style, and complexity. Yet he had treasured his correspondence with her immensely. At the end, though, he had noticed a difference. Her writing had become even simpler, and the text had become almost unreadable towards the very end. As if her decline in health and mind was being portrayed in the writing itself.

'I do not know what you will face at your destination, Jannus,' Mielle now said, interrupting his reverie and his remorse. She raised a hand at a certain point in the mist, and Jannus noticed that it had begun to dissipate somewhat. He looked around and also noticed that the last of the ghostly resonances seemed to have gone away.

'I do hope you find what you are looking for, dear Jannus.' She turned around with an enigmatic expression on her face. As the mist seemed to slowly disappear, so Mielle seemed more transparent; Jannus thought he could almost see *through* her. For some reason he could not explain, he held out the staff to her.

'Do you want this back, my lady? I did not mean to take it with me.'

She gazed at the staff, and then back at him. Then she gave him one final smile, just a slight upward pull of the lips, yet somehow affiliative.

'I do not need it, Jannus. Bring it with you to where you need to go. I suspect you might find a use for it before the end.'

CHAPTER XXII

Please, Give Answer

As Jannus started walking up the hill towards his childhood home, leaving the Plaza (mist-shrouded, yet again) behind him, he felt his chest tightening. It felt like one of the old panic attacks returning, and for a brief second, he was alarmed. All the catastrophic thoughts were on the verge of coming back.

But then the pain subsided somewhat, and he felt slightly relieved. He had started to use the staff as a walking supplement again on this last stretch of his journey, uphill. Jannus wondered if this was what Mielle had meant with "finding a use for it before the end." Somehow, he thought not. He kept his gaze fixed on the mansion.

This neighbourhood was populated with villas, and Jannus knew it as a mostly lucrative and expensive area of his home city. All the houses here were grand, and most of the properties were also larger in scale, as a whole, compared to most other neighbourhoods. This was the Upper Ward; truly, the only area remaining in his home town that could claim that title. None were as grand as the mansion that still stood above them all, though. He wondered, briefly, why all this was as he remembered. He *was* in the dreamscape still, right? Jannus looked around uncertainly, but the shadowed amethyst glow that covered his surroundings reassured him, if not exactly bringing him any comfort.

After a few hundred feet, Jannus felt his chest tighten again. And this time it remained, and spread. Suddenly, his whole body ached; it was a strange sensation, he thought. It was not a typical physical pain that he would have been quite familiar with. No, this was something else; like some sort of pressure burdening his physical shell, an outside (or maybe inside?) force or weight that threatened to bring him to his knees.

Despite himself, Jannus chuckled, still keeping his gaze fixed on the mansion, not paying too much attention to all the villas he passed, uphill. He had always found most things easy to circumvent; walking straight towards what he should be facing still proved a challenge. It looked to be the same thing this time around. As he got closer and closer, the weight on him from outside seemed to gain in substance, and he relied more and more on the quarterstaff to keep even a slow pace toward his end goal.

As an exercise (or escape, rather), Jannus thought of ways to distract himself. As per his own vocation for so many years, he tried to think of something else. The first subject of choice his consciousness seemed to come up with was thoughts of his former wife.

Jannus almost lost his grip on the staff while a mental image was conjured up in his mind. Yet something was different. Usually, images of her were mired in feelings of bitterness and regret, anger and anxiety. This time he remembered her vivacity, her brightness of character that was so unlike him at the time of their meeting. And he recalled her affability, yet again so unlike himself at any point in time; her way with people had seemed so natural, while Jannus himself really had to work at it. 'People just need time to get to you know, Jannus,' she had once told him, and so it had always been.

The few times he had worked in couple's counselling, one of the subjects that had emerged many times was the subject of similarities and opposites; which people are attracted and drawn to which people? He had never provided a universal answer. It was always individual, of course. But if he had to answer for himself, he would say that the latter had been at play with regard to himself and his former wife. But if the fact that they had been opposites had been the foundation of them starting their relationship, maybe it had also been the cause of their downfall. Maybe he really should have tried to see it from her perspective that final time.

Jannus passed a villa that he thought he recognised. A yellow-brick house, onyx-tiled roof, it was one of the largest villas he had passed so far. As a general rule, they became grander the further they were situated up the hill. This had been the home of one of his father's business associates. Jannus remembered that he had a son about the same age as himself. His father had invited his associate and his family to dinner at the mansion at one time, Jannus recalled. He had been about ten years old, the other boy maybe a year older. Jannus had had an immediate dislike of the slightly older boy. Back then, he had not understood quite why, until years later when it dawned on him that the other boy had looked much like himself. Or at least, how he thought other people might perceive him.

After he had passed the villa, Jannus stopped to gather his breath, still leaning on the staff. Other than his own breathing, the dreamscape was completely silent. The uphill street in the dreamscape had so far been fairly similar to the real-world street, he recalled from childhood memory. And just as that thought came to him, the view before him changed, *shifted,* as if being called to do so. A few houses changed colours, a few lost parts of themselves as if suddenly cut apart by something unseen, yet clean and sure in a way that left nothing behind. And now the houses around him *truly* appeared like he remembered, when he had walked here as a child.

As he stood there, regaining his composure, Jannus thought he heard other sounds emerge; first he thought it was his own heartbeat that must have struggled through the uphill-exertions. But then it seemed like the sound came from someplace else. Jannus realised that it *was* the sound of a heartbeat, a *pulse,* gaining in sound and strength, beating both harder and faster. For some reason he thought that it had started sometime before, but it was only now within frequency. Looking behind him, the Plaza had been enfolded in mist again, and thus beyond his sight. Yet in the silence he thought he could hear other sounds emerge from the shrouded heart; sounds of battle, shouting and screaming and crying, steel against steel.

Somewhat curious, Jannus kept listening until the sounds of battle died out; maybe the battle was done, or maybe the ghostly resonances just played out their final moments, their final trial. Whatever the nature of the mist-shrouded conflict, it turned his thinking towards what or *who* would be facing him ahead. Him, his client of the enigmatic smile; him of the wild stories, and the cold, unfeeling heart. Jannus recalled some of his former client's rather unbelievable stories concerning his possible backgrounds. One time he had been an important executive in an even more important company; another time he had presented himself as a traveller, a man of the world, as it were. At a particular session, he had even tried to convince Jannus that he had once been a member of the French Legion. 'They're still after me, Doc,' he had told him. 'Don't ya know it, they're still after me.' And then he had smiled his enigmatic smile, and let the session end.

Jannus did not look forward to seeing that mysterious smile again; from the way he remembered it, it had looked halfway alien, and halfway all-too-familiar.

He looked back up at the mansion. From here it looked even more decrepit than before; no one had maintained it for many years now, and the neglect was palpable. Yet it still stood there on its high hill. Part of him wanted to see it all crumble down and turn to dust; another part of him was fearful that it would be the last thing remaining. As Jannus resumed his walking, his thoughts turned from warfare and conflict to the man with the mirrored smile, to Mielle, and some of her words of premonition.

This will be your own battle, Jannus, she had warned him. *Your own battle, like you always dreamed. A true hero of the day. Are you truly ready for this, Jannus?* At this he had only shrugged, uncertain of the answer he thought she might want to hear. She had fixed her eyes on him in response, and he remembered how her anger had built; *You do not know?* Jannus remembered how Mielle had struggled to compose herself, and he recalled how he had wondered why this had been so important for her, to actually get mad at him.

After a while she had continued her warnings. *'We must be ready for our battles, Jannus.'* After this it had seemed like she had talked more to herself, than him, or maybe both of them. *'And beware treachery, Jannus. They never regarded me as supernal in any matters, in truth. Remember Alberigo?'* Jannus shook his head at this, but Mielle had not seemed to notice.

'Entombed forever in a lake of frost shimmering like glass, a lake of mirrors in truth. You grasp the edge with tooth and nail, Jannus, though it pains you to do so. You can never let go.' After this tirade, Mielle had breathed heavily, as if her words had taken great strength from her. *Not her words,* Jannus thought, as he approached the front gate to his childhood home. *But what they meant to her.*

Her very last words had been almost imperceptible. *'Love has no place any more, Jannus. The world has grown cold.'* Jannus had not agreed with her statement, but since the words had almost seemed to bleed out of her, he had not spoken out. Now that he opened the half-rusted iron gate, Jannus almost wished that he had. As for her words of being a "a hero of the day", he had not quite understood that either, to his present regret. True enough, as a boy he had often dreamed of all the heroic deeds he would like to perform (the most durable being saving himself and his mother). But how would Mielle have known about that? Besides, as he got older, he had forgotten most of those dreams, and been ashamed of the rest.

'To change from being someone's number-one zero to be their one in a million was not necessarily preferable either; he would not want someone to change someone from being absolutely negative to absolutely positive; either way could be just as damaging as the other.' Were those words his own? Had he heard them

from someone else? Jannus could not remember. But he *did* wonder, as he finally stood before his childhood home, broken and battered, yet still majestic and powerful, somehow, what they would all say if they could see him now? His mother? Father? Grandmother? Sister? Claire, his former wife? Johan of the Outer Isles? Mielle, the lady of the dreamscapes? *What would you say?* he wondered.

Standing outside his childhood home, Jannus thought it looked mostly familiar. Next to the front door was a wooden bench, some of the wood cracked from too much exposure. He still had memories, buried and locked away, of being sent out here for punishment, even in freezing winter. The snow had sometimes covered both him and bench before he was allowed inside, none the wiser in terms of whatever he might have done wrong.

And as Jannus finally opened the front door to his childhood home, he heard something shatter, and *break,* and for the briefest of moments he wondered whether it was the sound of the world breaking. And he entered a childhood hallway of mirrors, with his face displayed in every one of them, each one was slightly different from the others. And he saw himself, and all that lay beneath, all the hurt and the anger and the pain. And he saw who and what had been waiting in the mirror staring back at him in horror and delight in recognition. And the veil was gone and he saw himself and he reached out to embrace and comfort, gentleman and leisure both. To show himself that he finally understood, and the child must be seen and heard, and he learned he finally had the strength and the heart to reach out to the child, and then he felt the floor underneath crumble, and he went down and down and down.

CHAPTER XXIII

Enter the Drowned Nations: Into a Realm Eternal

I: THE RUINED DEEPS

He had entered the mansion, a place of dreams and childhood, and all the things became warped.

After what seemed like forever, Jannus finally raised himself to a standing position. He had apparently reached the bottom of... *something*. He had been falling and falling, and now, there was no room left for that. It had been like falling into a great sea with thunderous waves crashing this way and that. Jannus had tried to stay afloat, to no avail. No land in sight — only an empty horizon, as it ever had been. Overhead, thunder and lightning had ripped the sky apart, offering no comfort to his ever-tiring body.

Finally, his reserves had run out, and the drowning had begun. At first, Jannus had panicked. His life's memories had assaulted him frantically, his every hope and desire, his pains and his regrets, had all come crashing back into his mind. And yet the drowning had just continued, while he had felt... well, fine.

It had certainly *seemed* like he had been drowning, yet not quite. It had been more akin to lying in a bath with water flowing over you, back and forth, again and again, being prompted by your own movements while submerged. And his descent had continued into the deeps, into the dark, until he could see nothing at all. Along the way, he thought he might have closed his eyes, and lost consciousness. Until he woke up here, at the bottom, of wherever this was supposed to be.

As he reached the bottom, full of dirt and sand and mud, he looked up through a veil of water, about half a mile above him. But he was *below* the veil, the curtain of water. Yet not *in* water himself. A bluish-white light from above broke on the surface of the water.

Twisting his gaze away from the water-veil, Jannus looked about to see if he could see anything or anyone in his immediate vicinity. From what he could tell, it looked desolate. It was hard to tell, though.

The shadows were ever-deep here, almost impenetrable. There was a purple-black haze to everything, as if he was back in a dreamscape. Jannus got the sensation that it was more *real* than ever. And dangerous. Suddenly, a thought of what sounded like shuffling feet emerged from the shadows behind him.

Jannus twisted about, staff in hand. Momentarily surprised by the presence of the staff, he saw nothing before him. Only shadows. Focusing, Jannus thought there was a certain *presence* to the shadows. Not as if there was *someone* moving about in there. But more like the shadows themselves had some sort of direction to them. Or *intention,* maybe.

I'm scaring myself now, Jannus thought, and shook his head. And then he noticed something on the ground in front of him. Footsteps in the sand and dirt moving out of the shadows, and then back in again, it looked like, forming two lines of footsteps. Jannus did not need to lean closer to see that the imprint was not from a shoe or boot. But from someone who had bare feet.

Looking up again at the curtain of water, Jannus again noticed how the light seemed to break on the surface. Almost none of it reached down here; the shadows reigned here, and held sway. Somehow, he felt indebted to the small sliver of light left to him. Jannus got the sense that if that had not been there, he might have been left in complete darkness.

Glancing briefly again at the footsteps, Jannus gazed about to see if he could somehow tell if there were any places in the shadows surrounding him that were somehow different. Less, *substantial.* He was acutely aware that the direction he mostly focused on was opposite the location of the footsteps. Squinting, he thought he saw something, a pattern almost, or a shape. Maybe it was just hopeful thinking, but Jannus decided he might as well move forward. Carefully, naturally.

He noticed immediately that the shadows seemed to recede before him as he walked at a slow pace. Yet they never moved more than five or six feet away, and some strands even seemed to reach out to him, as if curious of his presence there. Walking along, Jannus suddenly felt like something was missing. An *absence,* somehow. Observant of his immediate surrounding, it took him a while to realise what it was. His backpack was gone. Jannus thought briefly of going back to the place where he had arrived here, but then thought better of it. He was not sure he could find it. Glancing over his shoulder, the shadows were just as close behind him as they were in front of him. In fact, he was surrounded.

Grieving the loss of his supplies, Jannus trudged on. Not that he had anything of particular value in there, yet it had been a trusty companion of sorts throughout his journey so far; a familiar and comforting presence always supporting him. In the beginning it had seemed like an extra weight to hold on to, a burden on his back. But maybe it had also helped him *gain* in strength, somewhat...

Holding the staff in both hands, Jannus kept walking through the shadows. Some of the shapes in the shadows he thought he had noticed before, now loomed closer. From this distance, it looked like a great hill, if not a mountain. *Or maybe an iceberg with jagged peaks,* he thought absently. Feeling slightly surer of himself and his choice of direction, Jannus picked up his pace, staff still in front of him. The shadows kept receding before him, and it even appeared they were moving further and further away, as if acknowledging or even *appreciating* his choices.

'Look at me, guessing at the motives of shadows,'

Jannus muttered. As the shadow-shades in front of him got closer and closer, Jannus found that he had to glance up once in a while, to reassure himself of the presence of the water-veil, and the small sliver of light allowed to him.

The staff also felt like a reassurance of sorts. He had yet to use it in any way other than a walking supplement, to *lean on,* whenever his out-of-shape reality had been made clear to him. But it was also as if he were carrying a piece of Mielle with him, in a strange way. Not that it had been hers, per se, but she *had* been the one to find it, and been excited about its revelation, there at the edge of the woods atop the southern hill.

And then she had apparently given it to him, just before they parted at the mists at the edge of town. Jannus could still not recall such an event, but maybe she had been subtle, or he might just have been unaware. The number of times he had been unaware of things in his immediate vicinity had been almost unbelievable. So, Jannus *supposed* that Mielle might have been able to put the staff into his hands while the mists covered them and she pushed him on. And yet... and yet.

A part of him had come to believe, or suspect, that Mielle might have been guiding him this whole time. Edging him on toward some destination that she had chosen for him. Certain pieces were beginning to fall into place, Jannus thought. His dreams and visions, the letter, the journey home. His presence *here,* at this very moment. A lot of it had begun to seem coordinated to

Jannus, as if some architect had drawn it all up beforehand, and then set it all into motion.

As the shadows receded further away, and the shapes became clearer (*not a mountain,* he thought. *And not an iceberg),* Jannus cursed at himself. He had wanted nothing more than to make a change here. Make some improvements in his life, turn things around, finally. Jannus had felt a sense of pride in his achievement, a sense of accomplishment.

Not that he thought he had done anything significant or extraordinary, by any means. Truly, he had only travelled what amounted to be a few days, fewer than a hundred miles. Most of those miles through fairly rough terrain, to be sure, but even so… Nothing extraordinary, or anything else he could have done.

Yet Jannus had still felt proud of what he had done. He had not known how it would end, but just the fact of him trying again. Something. Anything.

But now? What if the whole had been orchestrated? If this whole thing had not been his own purpose, but someone else's? He stopped in his tracks. Had Mielle lied to him? Kept his suspicions silent with her own guile and presence, or maybe by his own indecision? Despite himself, Jannus chuckled softly. He did not really know if this whole thing was real or not, or if it still was a kind of mad dream. Maybe he had fallen down into the basement of the old childhood mansion? It had looked dishevelled from the outside; maybe the inside of the house had been in disrepair and he had fallen through the woodwork?

It did not seem plausible to Jannus. But then, neither did his present circumstances. Maybe the key to the whole thing was that it was real enough, for him. And thus consequential. Whatever it was — derived from his tortured mind and soul — it still held meaning. There were still choices and truths to be made from this. Feeling somewhat resolute again, Jannus walked on until the shadows had parted completely, and he found himself standing before a ruined wonder.

Leaning the staff against his shoulder, Jannus was transfixed by the sight before him; an ancient city it appeared like, yet fallen, and far from its glory. Great golden pillars had been torn down and lay cracked on the pavement. In their place stood towers of crimson and obsidian, looking terrible and beautiful, both. Those most have been the "mountains" he had seen from afar, while surrounded by the shadows. Though from here, they looked nothing like mountains, nor icebergs with jagged peaks. Most of the buildings had also been turned to rubble, leaving no doubt as to the fate of the former inhabitants. It looked like some great disaster had struck this place; maybe a natural disaster, or maybe a great conflict had struck her. Whatever it had been, it had been merciless.

Moving slowly, Jannus walked down a ruined street, being careful of his steps. He found himself looking inside the houses, which was not of any great difficulty; there were hardly any walls left, so what was left was mostly just rubble; a pile of white stonework, bereft of its former elegance. He noticed that the shadows, purple and back, seemed to have retreated to these ruined buildings, almost covering the rubble as a layer of protection. Jannus was no expert on architecture, nor history, for that matter, yet this place looked truly *old*. As if it had been part of some lost civilisation. Even so, it was easy to imagine the majesty this place might once have had, back when the golden pillars had stood tall. Now, the crimson and obsidian made their mark on what was left.

Ahead of him, Jannus noticed that one of the buildings was still standing, somewhat intact. It had been built with white bricks, and a red roof. Apart from a man-sized hole in the roof, and dark marking on one of the walls as if from fire damage, it looked relatively unharmed.

Feeling some amount of trepidation, Jannus moved closer. He stood ten or twelve feet from what might once have been the front door, yet he could see nothing inside. A veil of purple and black covered the entrance, and blocked his sight. Despite his curiosity, Jannus did not move any closer. He wanted to, but could not; it made him feel cowardly, but that was not enough to motivate him forward. As he prepared to move on deeper into the ruined city, Jannus heard a voice.

'Anybody seen my baby?' someone called, out of the dark.

Mielle gasped for breath, and had to stop. She had been running for what had seemed like an eternity. They were so close now. Only a sliver of hope was left to them, yet opportunity remained. She had been moving ahead of Jannus, hastily, in the ruins. Oh, how she remembered the glory of this place; where the people had seen the light for the first time, and where people smiled to each other in the streets, with no fear or alarm. Where children had laughed, and the bells had rung, their harmonies ever enfolding the people within their hearing, in the wonder that had been Solis Brumalis. Forever after known as Cordolium, after Mielle and her people had conquered the place.

II: SHADOWS OF THE PAST

'Anybody seen my baby? Anybody seen her?'

Startled, Jannus turned around, staff once again held in front of him, defensively. Before him, stood a woman in ragged, grey clothing, wild-haired and wide-eyed. She stood in the doorway. Jannus noticed that she had bare feet, and for a moment wondered if she had been the one earlier, leaving the prints. Somehow, he thought not.

The woman looked at him with eyes that looked half-afraid, half-crazed. Jannus held his stance for a few moments more, then felt foolish, and let down his guard. The strange woman took a cautious step forward. Jannus thought she appeared emaciated, and starved. He also noticed that the woman had cuts on arms and legs, some of them only partly healed.

Has someone attacked her? Jannus wondered. *Or are they self-inflicted?* Somehow, he thought these were not the right questions to ask.

'I mean no harm,' he finally managed. The woman only stared at him, not approaching further. *Would I, in her case?* Jannus thought, sympathetically. He tried to smile at her. 'Truly, I mean no harm.' The woman had not changed her expression, or stance, at all. Then a thought occurred to him. 'I come in peace, as they say,' and then shifted his grip on the staff, so that he held it horizontally in both hands, as if offering it to her.

That seemed to make a difference to the woman; she did not smile back at him, but nodded at him, and held two fingers (one broken nail, the other nail blackened) to her eyes.

'Peace is welcome, stranger,' she said, whispering, as if afraid for someone else to hear. For the first time, Jannus realised how *silent* everything was here. There no other people here besides the two of them; none that he could see, anyway. Nor was there any kind of noise or the usual bustle one associated with a city.

Well, of course not, you fool, he thought. *If there were ever any kind of "bustle" in this place, it is long since gone.*

'As I said, I do not mean any harm,' Jannus reiterated to the woman. 'In fact, I do not quite know where I am.' He was vaguely aware that his words were slightly similar to those he had first uttered to Mielle.

The woman in front of her reminded him of someone. Not Mielle, of course. Their dispositions were entirely different, and whatever situation Mielle might find herself in, Jannus could not imagine her with the same demeanour as this woman. Even when Mielle had looked dishevelled in certain dreamscapes, she had almost always maintained her composure. Thoughts of Mielle now filled him with anger and disappointment, both at her *and* himself.

This woman in front of him appeared to have lost her composure long ago. She had still not spoken any word since her words of peace and welcome. Jannus thought of another approach.

'Do you need any help?'

She tilted her head at him, as if not understanding his inquiry.

That particular movement, together with her looks, reminding Jannus of someone. It was not in the hair or the ragged clothes. Mostly the eyes, and the *look* in there. He thought he might have seen that before. A former client, maybe? No. *Closer* than that.

'Can I do anything for you? Are you in need of aid?' Jannus tried again. He felt some of his sympathy waning for the strange woman, and then, immediately, recriminated himself for it. Then he noticed something else. It was not *completely* silent here. A low drone, almost below the edge of hearing, emanated from somewhere. It was very indistinct, almost deliberately so. He had difficulty ascertaining the source of the sound, though, since it seemed to permeate everything in its subtle ways.

Then Jannus looked to the towers, crimson and obsidian, high above, and it clicked. For some unknown reason, the sound appeared to emanate from those, like a very slow pulse, creating an endless, low-frequency sound. A pulse. *Or like a beating heart, almost still,* Jannus thought.

'Have you seen my baby?' the woman now asked him, repeating her initial questions.

'No, madam, I am sorry to say I have not,' he commiserated. 'Maybe she went off someone, on her own?'

The woman shook her head, not angrily, only despondent. 'Nay, she cannot. She is but a babe.'

Jannus felt foolish, once again. The woman *had* called out for her baby, after all. Suddenly it struck him who the woman reminded him of. The look in her eyes, the tilt of her head, when something had been beyond her understanding. His sister.

The strange woman and his estranged sister. Now that he had made the connection, it was almost uncanny. In fact, more and more of the woman's features made him recall his sister all over again, though they had not met or spoken for many years.

Jannus barely remembered the last time they had spoken. Or what they had spoken of. He could only recall the feeling, the embarrassment, the anger, and the accusations (unwarranted, from both sides, he knew now) that had torn asunder what had remained of their relationship. *You left me!* she had shouted at him. *You left me behind. You forgot about me! You promised. You promised, and yet you left me.* He had not even tried to defend himself against those last words. It was true enough. At a crucial time in their lives, he had gone on ahead, sought his own fortune, and tried to forget most of what had gone before. Including her.

And he had mostly succeeded, to be sure. Jannus had moved away from home, pursued his education, and had a somewhat successful career with its own share of accolades. Most of them packed away in a box somewhere, but still, they had been honestly earned, at the time. Concerning his private life, he at least had the fortune of one longer-lasting relationship of worth, which he still, at least in moments of levity, cherished.

Now looking at this strange woman in front of him, seemingly in need of aid, he felt conflicted. He could stay here and figure things out, yet he had the notion that whatever he sought was somewhere beyond this point. Not here with this woman of no significance.

And there it is, Jannus. Leaving someone behind, yet again. Hiding away when someone is in need, tending to yourself, only.

The woman had not moved away from her initial position, nor spoken a word. But she kept looking about, as if searching for something. *Her baby, naturally,* Jannus thought. For a second he wondered if the woman might be maddened indeed. But then the old familiar theory asserted itself, and the realisation came that this woman might be in shock.

'My lady,' Jannus started, now having decided how to move forward. The woman seemed to have relaxed somewhat, since she was no longer keeping her eyes fixed on him. He took that to be a good sign; she must no longer see him as an immediate threat to her safety. *So far, so good,* he thought, congratulating himself. *Take your victories where you can.*

'I do not know where your baby is, I'm afraid. I do not believe she is here, however.' The woman looked at him, puzzled, yet attentive. Jannus still kept his distance; he was making progress, but wanted to maintain it.

'She would most likely have heard you by now, don't you think? When she heard you calling?'

The woman gave a slight nod. And then, 'Aye. Aye, she would have.' Jannus did not know how long the woman might have called upon her baby, in vain, yet she seemed surprised and slightly disturbed at the revelation.

'Maybe you could come with me, my lady. Then we'll search for her, together?'

It was gamble, he knew. If the woman was truly in shock, regarding whatever had happened here, her faith in strangers could very well be diminished, if not non-existent. The destruction around them appeared to have happened a long time ago, yet the woman in front of him seemed to be affected by something that had happened *recently.* Jannus recalled that Mielle had once told him something about the nature of these dreamscapes; that time and space worked differently here, not entirely logical or reasonable to our understanding.

The woman had not reached out to his proposal. When it looked like she was not going to, Jannus made ready to leave, slightly disappointed in himself that he had not been able to help someone, yet again.

After three or four steps, he heard her call out. 'Good sir!' He turned around. The woman, who so resembled his sister, had taken a few steps forward, arms crossed. 'Your words make sense, I believe. My baby, wherever she is, will not be found here.' She stopped a few feet in front of Jannus, and looked up at him. *Her height too, or thereabouts,* he thought, slightly worried at all the similarities.

'I want to travel with you, sir, to your destination, wherever it is. Maybe I will find her on the way.' He nodded at her, and made his way back to what seemed like the main thoroughfare through this part of the broken city, the woman always walking just behind him.

They passed through three gates following the thoroughfare, each one grander than the last. Jannus had pointed each of them out to the woman, yet she had not seemed interested. The arched gates appeared to be the only structures around here that were not broken in any way. He could imagine the banners and flags that must have flown here. Jannus wondered if the gates had been made of any kind of special building material that whatever force had struck had not been able to destroy. He thought to ask the woman coming with him, but then decided against it.

Despite her silence, Jannus felt good about bringing her along. Or at least, not leaving her behind. And he also felt a strange sense of satisfaction that whatever had transpired throughout this whole endeavour, he had still managed to struggle on; he had not turned about, and returned home. He was moving forward into the unknown. Jannus did not know where he had found his courage; maybe, if this had not been a dreamscape, his every step would be halted by anxiety or thoughts of a depressive nature that would weigh him down. Anxiety had a tendency to make every step a struggle, and so it had been with his depression, as well. The difference between the two had been this: in the former, the struggle had revolved around the thought that something terrible would happen before you got to wherever you needed to go. And in the latter case, the struggle concerned the notion of whether or not it would really matter if you reached your goal.

Maybe this place, whatever and wherever it is, actually helps me? Jannus thought hopefully, as they left the third and last gate behind them, entering what looked to be the city centre. The woman kept calling out to her baby along the way. No one answered.

Mielle had been chased by her own shadows; her robes ripped to shreds by their incessant clawing. They were the terrors of her past, people she had left behind, or chased away. None of the shadows wore faces, yet she knew them all. Things were moving too fast now, her own past catching her off-guard at a moment's weakness. She had been too intent on making sure everything went as it should, and then disregarded her own safety. Of course, this was a new experience to her; never had she tried to go back and undo one of her mistakes. She had always kept moving forward, ever expanding, ever conquering. And then, when she had lost it all, she kept holding onto even the thinnest threads of what remained, or what reminded her of what she had once held in her grasp. Another shadow tried to claw her, and Mielle evaded it, as best she could. Not entirely successful, though, since she felt another flaming lash on her legs. Jannus' goal was most important now, her own safety only worth something until the goal was reached. After that, it did not matter to Mielle. Or almost not. She still retained a tiny sliver of hope that some future would be open to her. She almost evaded another claw.

III: A HERO OF THE DAY

The centre consisted of a great plaza; most of the buildings here were only rubble, with a few exceptions. Four main roads led out of the plaza, leading to other parts of the city. Standing in the middle of the plaza, Jannus suddenly developed the notion that they were being watched, observed, and not kindly. His companion had not spoken, but remained silent, eyes downcast. She had stopped calling out for her baby.

Suddenly, people started to appear; some of them from the buildings that were yet standing, others appeared from behind corners, and it even looked like someone emerged from the rubble itself. These latter ones were mostly children, small enough to find shelter even amidst the broken stone. It was with an aching heart, that Jannus noticed his shadow-sister looking hopefully at the children, to see if any one of them might be her baby, and then looking dejected, when none of them met the criteria.

The people — dressed like his companion, in grey rags mostly — kept their distance. Jannus noticed that a few of them carried staffs like his own, but with one end sharpened to resemble spears. He was not especially fearful of these strangers, since they, again like his companion, mostly seemed emaciated. *But maybe, as a consequence, also desperate,* Jannus thought, feeling just a little bit weary.

A few of the elders approached him, a man and a woman, both spear-wielders. They stopped about twelve feet in front of Jannus. The woman looked as if she wanted to say something, but something held her back. The man only squinted at him, as if wanting to reassure himself of their presence, or *reality*. The rest of the ragtag group had gathered together, another ten or twelve feet behind the two elders.

Finally, as silence had been stretched out unbearably, the elder man spoke. 'You carry the mark, stranger, yet dress like one unaware'. The man stopped talking, as if awaiting answer to the cryptic preamble. When Jannus did not respond, the man grimaced, and nodded at the quarterstaff in Jannus' hands. 'You carry the mark of those who guarded the path by the ancient writ.'

The woman moved forward, a few steps in front of the other elder, and made a half-bow to Jannus. 'Welcome to Bright Haven, stranger. Welcome to our shelter, caught between light and dark. We are those who remain.'

A greeting of some sort? Their demeanour helped Jannus relax somewhat, though he was unfamiliar with their customs. They still seemed wary of him, but no more than he was of them.

'I thank you,' he managed, trying his way forward. 'I am humbled by your greeting.' To Jannus, that seemed like something that was right to say. 'I come in peace,' he emphasised. His companion had responded well to *that* one.

The two elders nodded at him, as if in confirmation of his words, and gestured the rest of the group forward. A few maintained their places, but most shuffled forward, all holding hands as if afraid of getting lost from one another.

'Here we are gathered, stranger,' the elder man began. 'The survivors and refugees of the great conflict that has plagued these lands for a generation.' The man gestured around them. 'We are the remains,' he repeated. Jannus thought he sounded tired and despondent. *Maybe he has told the story too many times,* Jannus wondered. *Or lived it too long?*

The elder woman picked up the tale with much greater exhortation than her elder companion. 'We sharpened our spears with great fastidiousness, and learned to throw them with precision. When the enemy came from behind their wall of ice, everything changed with merciless vicissitude.'

The elder woman had stepped closer and closer to Jannus until she stood right in front of him. He was more than a head higher than her, yet she still had a fierce, commanding presence. *She is leading these remains,* Jannus thought.

'We battled in the deep with creatures of water and light, against creatures of shadow, our human hearts ever entwined, a battle within and without. Soon we battled ourselves, as well, until we are those you see here today.'

The elder woman gestured to the group behind her, all of them now looking directly at Jannus. Feeling slightly alarmed at their attention, he calmed down when he noticed the nature of their regard. They were not aggressive, or hostile in any way. They seemed apprehensive, yes — but also, and curiously, *hopeful.*

One child, maybe aged seven or eight, stepped forward. Jannus saw she was carrying a small rock in one hand, as if holding a pet or maybe a stuffed bear. She looked up at him, utterly unafraid. 'Are you here to help us, sir?'

Dumbfounded, Jannus did not know what to say. *Help? Him? How? With what?* The group and the elders were still looking at him. Even his shadow-sister had left her own world for a while, to regard him sideways.

Looking about, as if seeking an escape, Jannus gazed around the ruined plaza. As before, most of what he saw had been turned to rubble. Yet something had *changed.* He now saw smoke emanate from some of the destruction around him, as if the damage had just been done. Now it looked more like the immediate ramification after an attack.

'Are you here to help us, sir?' the child asked once again, this time a bit more fearful with a revealing tremble in her voice.

Again, the doubts in his mind re-emerged. *Help? Him? Preposterous!* Jannus recalled one of his old teachers, who would usually remark with dark sarcasm on all the things he had not managed to say, or answer.

'Would you say anything, Jannus? Would you say anything at all?'

And then shame would hold him back, despite knowing the answer, and he would keep it inside, locked away where no one would see. And yet it stayed there, *remained...* oh how it remained and grew and grew, until he had felt ready to rage, and scream, and let everybody know that he *did* know the answer; he *did* know a way forward, a destination.

Jannus just never held any belief he would ever manage to reach it. Never shone in what he did, never showed anything with great ardour.

And yet… and yet… he looked up at what passed for a sky here in the dreamscape, the veil of water, a pale star behind it, now flickering. The group before him flinched every time the star faltered. He felt the girl grab his hand, and put her rock into it. She did not ask him again for help, but stepped back to the group.

Whether it was his own journeys, the nature of the dreamscape, or the girl's simple gift, Jannus felt that something was different. He still had doubts whether he would be able to help these people, whatever they needed from him. He still felt unequal, and *vulnerable.* Yet there was a strength hidden in that vulnerability that Jannus had not been aware of before. A *bravery* of sorts.

Jannus put the rock in his pocket, which made the girl smile, and nod. The two elders in front of him still appeared apprehensive, the elder man especially, while the woman held her steady gaze on him.

'Aye,' Jannus managed, his voice more emotional than he was prepared for. 'I'll do what I can to help you. What do you need of me?'

The elder man answered him, his voice still somewhat despondent, yet with a hint of *anger* underneath. 'We tried to stem the tide, sir. We tried to fight against the overwhelming force. They were the enemy, yet the fear was already there. We looked for our allies, the ones sworn to us by our ancient writ, yet no one came to our call. They never came, yet not because of courage lost.'

The elder man's voice had been gaining in strength as he gave his answer. And Jannus was shocked to see tears streaming down the man's face. Jannus realised, for the first time, how much the man had tried to hold back, trying to retain some semblance of dignity in front of his peers.

'And the people who served us and put their faith in our leadership, did not prove strong enough to stem the tide. Their spears did not pierce the heavy shields of the enemy, their armour remained impenetrable. Yet our people were not to blame for us. They did what they were told to believe. They did only what they were told to do.'

The elder man no longer looked at Jannus, his eyes downcast, as if in shame. The elder woman put her hand on the man's shoulder, her eyes sympathetic.

'Tell me, stranger,' the elder man said, in a voice no more than a whisper, yet loud and clear with grief and sorrow. 'Tell me where blame has fallen. Tell me where the fault lies.'

Jannus, his own heart now full of sympathy and understanding for the elder's plight, laid a hand on the man's other shoulder. 'In *your* eyes', Jannus told him, 'the blame and fault is *yours.*'

And for the first time, the elder man smiled at Jannus, while tears streamed down his face. Jannus felt his own eyes water in response. The elder woman still looked at the man, providing what comfort she could.

And then the sky cracked open, the human heart burst, and light and dark poured forth. And the pale star looked on without mercy, flickering and faltering, as the remains of the drowned nations sought shelter beneath the rubble.

Jannus felt himself stagger, shaken by the cacophony above and within his own heart, in shadow, flickering, yet finding resolve to stand ready against whatever had approached.

Mielle was crawling; the shadows had been relentless in their assault, and her defences had finally been broken. She almost could not see, blood streaming down her face like crimson tears. 'Deservedly so,' she thought bitterly, as she kept crawling. Only one shadow remained with her — no longer attacking, only following. She did not know where the other shadows had gone. Maybe they thought she was done, leaving only one for the kill? But they had underestimated her, as so many had done before. They had never understood the will that was her. Still, Mielle was tired, and she felt some measure of relief, when she saw she was near the top of the tower. The two ancient war-machines still stood since those fateful days, the pride of the empire. They still made their presence known, a reminder of what had passed here, long ago. Mielle had to go to the apex of both towers to achieve what she needed. What she had to accomplish. Jannus had met the remains of the inhabitants here, and they had seen in him someone who could provide them with salvation. As she had known they would. The only thing remaining was that Jannus would also see that in himself. And Mielle had to ascend both towers, or it would not be enough, whatever Jannus might or might not do. She was only near the apex of the first tower. And she was already tired.

IV: THIS SAVAGE COLD STAR

'Come to me, brightest of the Seraphim!' the foremost of the light shades bellowed, as they charged ahead to face their foes. The latter, creatures of darkness with cowled wings of flame and tears of blood, stood their ground and awaited the assault. Jannus knew that they had been entrapped at the earth's centre, where the daystar never shone its light, and whatever light they met they faced with righteous fury.

Jannus was standing guard before a few of the people from the plaza who had not had the time to get to shelter. Among them, his shadow-sister, and the child who gave him the rock, which he had secured in his pocket. He did not actually know what to do if any of the shades — light or dark — would come their way. So far, the shades appeared to be content in battling one another, leaving Jannus and his charges unharmed. He was not even sure who he was supposed to root for here. Part of him thought the light shades looked to be protectors of sorts, yet the way they fought the shades seemed utterly with mercy, and they wreaked havoc and destruction around them without filter, or thought of consequence. And the dark ones with wings of flame, while fierce, seemed to stand more on the defending side of things, never attacking of their own volition, but also relentless when the clashes became imminent.

Maybe they are both right, Jannus thought, as he observed the battle, neither side seeming to get the upper hand. He moved slowly backwards, with his two charges behind him, towards one of the last remaining buildings on the plaza. Just when they got close, two of the creatures — one light and dark — changed direction in mid-battle, and came into their vicinity, perilously close.

'Stay back!' Jannus shouted to his charges, not actually watching to see if they listened or not. This close, the creatures — the shades — were almost faceless, with no discernible features Jannus could recognise.

Not immediately, anyway. Yet there was something about them, he thought, while trying to keep a comfortable distance to the shades. Something strangely familiar, absurd as it seemed.

Suddenly, the two creatures stopped simultaneously, now facing Jannus instead of each other. They did not have the features to actually smile, but Jannus got the sense that they did. Holding the staff in front of him —

still not having any idea how to wield it as a weapon — he managed, somehow, to block their blows. They appeared to be working in tandem, now, as if against a common enemy. They charged again, and he managed to block, but had to retreat a couple of steps from the force of their blows.

Another charge, another block, a few steps back. They changed their charge mid-attack, and he blocked only one of them this time. He did not feel any pain, but something wet was running down his right leg. Jannus felt dizzy, and he knew it was only a matter of time before they got to him, as long as they worked together to fight him. *None of them are on our side*, he realised, much too late.

Another charge, another failed block, and he could hold the staff only in one hand. Out of breath, and out of time, Jannus prepared himself for the final assault. He closed his eyes, and heard someone beside him scream.

Crawling up the second tower with only one remaining eye, and most of the fingers on her left hand burned off, proved to be of great difficulty to Mielle. The first tower and what she had faced at the apex, had almost done her in.

And yet she persevered, because she had to. She could sense Jannus faltering, and so she had to go on. The last shadow had left her, almost dancing in the air above her as if gleefully celebrating her demise. And maybe it should. After all, the shadows were the true remains of those who had been left behind, spirits of vengeance of sorts, come to collect. And Mielle would be the greatest prize of them all, being the prime culprit, the architect and orchestrator of their demise.

Mielle did not blame them. She could not, at this point.

At the top of the obsidian stairs, she found what she was looking for; a bright, burning heart, at least triple the size of her head. Smoke emanated from the chambers as cold fire burned through it. It still beat, a pulse remained, yet at a lethally slow pace.

Yet Mielle knew that the heart would keep burning, and the flame would never perish, and thus, the suffering would continue until nothing would remain: thus was their design and intent. Mielle knew that she had to reach through the flames into the inner chambers of their heart with her one functioning hand. Her vision was unclear, hazy, as she reached in. Then everything went dark.

The battle was over. Jannus was on his back, still hurting from his wounds, but otherwise conscious.

He had not witnessed the end of the battle of light and dark. However, since he was still alive, and there was only silence, he assumed it was over. Jannus did not know who had been the victor, and neither did he care. *Had any one of them truly been in the right?*

Looking up, Jannus saw that the sky was clear, and the water-veil was gone. He wondered if it had been destroyed in the battle, or if there were any other explanation for its absence. The sun above shone brighter than before, not looking through a curtain of water. Though, from down here, in the drowned nations, it looked more like a cold star, savage and devoid of warmth and soul, infant in its promise of redemption. And Jannus looked within his own heart, grown cold, and grown lonely. Almost without soul. Yet, something was still there, still beating, a faint light flickering, trying to gather strength, and find its life, yet again.

Jannus got up into a sitting position. Looking around the plaza, it was still a ruin, but still with the same few buildings standing. And something was just a bit off, he thought. It took him a few moments to realize what it was, exactly. The plaza was still characterized by its destruction and its rubble. But it appeared old again, as if whatever harm had been done to it had been done long ago in the past, and not by some recent conflict.

Curious, he stood up. Trying to find his balance took him a while, as a bout of dizziness came upon him. It seemed like he had lost his staff again. Maybe it had broken in a last desperate attempt to guard himself. He was unsure.

A sudden voice called out. Jannus looked this way and that, at first unable to locate it. The voice called out again. He found his companion, she who had called out to her baby, and yet never found it. She lay in a ruined building, resting her back upon a wall that was reduced to rubble. She still wore her grey rags, and her face was bloodied. Her arms wore cuts as well, as if she had been defending herself. Or someone else, part of his mind mused.

Despite her appearance, the woman smiled when she saw him. Jannus knelt down by her side.

More than ever, he thought, she resembled his sister. Not because of her state, naturally, but because of her smile. Most of Jannus' recollections of his sister were long gone, but he would forever remember that smile. She had called him 'her gentleman of leisure', for some obscure reason he never found out. He had been her protector once, until he was not.

The woman now before him appeared to move in and out of consciousness, sometimes acting as if she was not truly there, and the next moment it seemed like she was very aware, and present. In these moments, she smiled at him, as if greeting an old acquaintance.

'I'm sorry,' Jannus started, not knowing where to go from there. 'I'm sorry,' he repeated, and took one of her hands in his. He felt her squeeze his hand, as she tried to make eye contact with him, but failed. She pointed at the sky.

'Look there,' she said in a voice just above a whisper, and Jannus obliged. 'It looks pale, does it not?' she said, echoing Jannus' own thoughts. 'It must be blind to our troubles, here in the deep. Still, it shines on, cold and merciless, as we are forgotten here in this savage life.'

Jannus did not look up at the star above, but kept focusing on the woman. That was the least he could do for her. Another one I could not save, he thought, self-recriminating. Maybe she sensed his state of mind, since she raised her other hand to his cheek.

As Jannus succumbed to his own exhaustion, he heard her last remaining words on her dying breath.

'Do not weep for me, stranger,' she said. 'I think I found my baby, my prince of the universe. I think… I think… I can hear his song.'

CHAPTER XXIV

Sleeping Softly, a Door Found

Jannus woke up early on Tuesday morning, fresher than he had felt forever. *Rescind that,* he thought, as an ache in his lower back made its presence known, when he rose from his bed. It looked as though he had fallen asleep atop the duvet last night.

It should have been a cold night, since it was late summer, and judging by all the rain over the last few weeks, autumn was already quickly underway. Looking at the imprint on the bed, Jannus had apparently fallen asleep almost in the middle of it, enjoying all the space and comfort of the double bed. He had not even closed the shades before falling asleep, and the early morning rays of light from the daystar found their way inside his bedroom. *Maybe that's why I'm an early riser today,* he wondered, putting on a pair of jeans, and a simple white shirt.

Looking around his bedroom, Jannus found that while everything was not exactly super-clean, it was fairly tidy and ordered; at least, from the chaotic view of someone who did not encompass the highest standards in such matters.

Jannus made his way through the living room to open the garden door, to let some of that fresh, morning air into his life-space. He stood there in silence for a few minutes, just enjoying the moment in time. He sauntered around in the back garden, and felt the grass between his toes, enjoying the sensation. Jannus felt appreciation at this quiet moment in time. He had even thought about making a kitchen garden again, to get his own supplies for cooking purposes. It felt like a thing both very new and very old to yet again have his feet (and hands) *connected* to the ground.

Jannus made his way to the kitchen to make his morning brew, still a routine-job every day. *We must have some sins,* he mused. Some nature or gardening programme was playing on the television, as he walked by it. Jannus did not even notice the open cupboard on his way to the kitchen; a cupboard now bereft from its former liquid secrets.

In the kitchen he smiled when he saw that he must have prepared for the morning coffee the night before; he had only to push the button to begin the process.

'I must be getting better,' Jannus chuckled as he looked outside his kitchen window.

The old widow next door and her daughter would come by later this evening. Jannus had planned to make dinner for them, maybe Cottage Pie (the old man's favourite he seemed to recall). He just wanted to thank the old lady for an old kindness done, for being there for him in the moment of her own mourning.

It was not that he had turned to a brave new world, exactly, or that he had embarked on a completely new life. *I still have too much up-neck cynicism for that,* he thought wryly, while the coffee machine behind him began coughing.

But he *did* feel more whole, in a way, and more complete than before. That he had to admit, despite the cynicism still prevailing from time to time. Doubts still remained. It was not a state of bliss; it was more a matter of being content — a more realistic way forward, somewhat.

As he poured himself his first mug of coffee of the day, Jannus could not help but chuckle again. *"Realistic." Really?* He was very much cognisant of the irony of the term, considering how he had reached this particular frame of mind. Mystical dreamscapes did not immediately lend themselves to the notion of being "realistic".

Jannus sat down on one of the kitchen chairs, and put his legs up to rest on the other one. The kitchen table was empty of newspapers. He did not keep up with the news that much any more, at least not on a day-to-day basis. He did not feel the need any more; no need to enhance the feeling of being just a little bit behind every day. Instead, there was a half-finished puzzle laid out on the table. Eight hundred pieces total, about four hundred to go. When it was done, it was supposed to look like a waterfall in the distance, with a couple of people standing on a nearby ledge, looking and pointing at said waterfall.

Jannus had never been much for puzzles in truth. He never had the patience for it. But a couple of weeks ago he had made an impulse purchase and bought it anyway. Even though it had been slow (very slow!) work, Jannus found that he had enjoyed himself with it so far, much to his own surprise.

For so long he had been looking for egress, for a way out of life. Jannus had given up much of himself on his journey. But in requital, Jannus felt he had gained something more. Still unknown, yet undefined, to be sure. He could no longer consider himself sophomoric, at least in most matters.

Jannus knew that he still had something of an edge to him. A *sharpness* in his personality and voice that affected people around him in different ways. And himself, naturally. Jannus did not want to lose that particular trait. He just wanted to learn how to *wield* it differently. He would like to do more than just persevere, and no longer do so only in perfect isolation.

Jannus felt himself getting slightly irritated at the puzzle before him, so he put down the two pieces he had in his hand, took his mug, filled it up again, and made his way to the garden.

Though he still lived in the suburbs, Jannus thought the garden had a certain bucolic quality to it. The morning dew still covered the chairs in the garden, so he spent a few moments wiping one of them off as best he could with his free hand. Sitting down, Jannus realised he could have done a better job; he felt his jeans getting soaked in certain places.

Jannus started to feel irritated, edging on angry, but then he smiled, and laughed and laughed and laughed. He laughed until he was almost out of breath, and his sides hurt. Just before he recovered, he suddenly noticed that his shirt had also become soaked from the remains of the morning dew, and then the laughter resumed.

Jannus finally made a true, and *lasting* recovery. Almost miraculously, he had not lost a single drop of coffee. Enjoying another sip, he looked up at the sky. The daystar did not burn too brightly this early in the morning. At least not in his eyes; not any more. As he enjoyed the daystar's gentle caress, Jannus thought he suddenly saw some coruscations — dark purple and silver black — emerge from the daystar above. But then he blinked, and they had disappeared, as if they had never been.

A small reminder of what have been, Jannus, a recognisable voice echoed in his mind, still gentle, yet somehow hardened. *And of what might still be.*

And Jannus leaned back, morning dew be damned, and closed his eyes, as he felt the daystar's light gain in strength, and he welcomed its return. And his own.

And the past retained its own echoes, the memories still had a place, not locked away any more, but had instead chosen a place of comfort. And the neighbours looked forward to spending their time with him, to his surprise, yet not theirs. And Mother looked on with sad, darkened eyes, still giving all she could. And Father looked on with discerning eyes of hard, grey steel, yet with an iron pride, buried deep, gazing at his son. And Grandmother still looked on with her gentle smile, wise in the ways of the world. A sister still estranged, true, yet with a bright shadow who still endured. And Johan of the Outer Isles travelled the highways of the world, ever moving from place to place, somehow bringing his home with him everywhere he went. And the gentleman of leisure had finally become the hero he had always wanted. Giving away his own warmth, as he received some in return, not being left cold. And the high lady of the dreamscapes kept her vigil as was her punishment due, her exile self-chosen to carry burdens of past failures. As if noticing his regard, the collie at her feet raised his head and looked back at him, as if reassuring him that she was somehow at peace, or content with her own choice, at the very least. And that they had both found a way forward; a path, a doorway. Still with their own uncertainties, to be sure.

Maybe they would meet once again on the journey ahead of them. Where, he could not say. In dreams, maybe? Or in his waking hours? Or maybe they would always be beyond sight until the final hour, until that sunny day where they would find their end. Until then, they would live, and live as best they could.

EPILOGUE

Maravilloso Sonido

Claire was looking at three people on a wooden bench, each playing their guitars, kids playing on the grass beside them.

Walking through the park on a cloudy day. She had wanted to go these last few days, but a lot of things got in the way, as usual; as ever, it was hard to find the time for all the things she wanted to do. Claire would never have thought she would get this far in life. A healthy relationship, and with a child on the way, and everything!

She had not yet learned to live as if every day was ineffable, but she tried to make the most of it, at least. In her own view, she had also become less intransigent. Claire had never been particularly decorous either, nor had she ever had any inclination to be.

But hey, a person can change, right? she thought, as she caught sight of one of the wild cats that roamed the park. They were mostly unseen in daytime, though they made sure of their presence at nighttime, much to the chagrin of the people living close by.

This particular one was lying, indolent, in the shade

of a great oak tree. The cat blinked slowly at her, when it noticed her looking at it. Claire blinked back at the cat. It reminded her of her own cat at home; a true rogue who knew how to charm his way around her. She was not fooled, though: she was very well acquainted with his obstreperous nature when the sun went away, and he roamed through the night.

A family of four passed by her on the gravelled path; she nodded at them, but they were preoccupied by their own dynamics.

Heh, dynamics, she thought, shaking her head while she chose the right turn on the path. A true "Jannus" word if there ever was on. She often thought of him these days, and of how he might be doing. Jannus had actually been very loving, but also ever-striving, and not willing to let go. And that could be a great strength; at other times it was a burden on their relationship. Claire would not have described him as belligerent — not exactly — but closed-off and stubborn to a fault.

She had ever doubted herself, but Jannus had actually helped her realise so much about herself; both in terms of what was right for her in life, but also what was wrong. That Jannus himself turned out to be one of the wrong elements of her life was almost a side-note by now. Claire still felt a certain amount of empathy.

She truly hoped the best for her old comrade-in-arms, wherever he was in life.

Claire hoped he had found his peace, as she had

found hers. She still considered herself a work-in-progress in certain ways, but overall, she was satisfied with her current life. She had not quite reached her life ambitions, privately or in terms of work, but Claire felt like she was well underway.

She grimaced. "I felt like"… Jannus had always corrected her in that, and tried to explain to her the difference between "feeling" and "thoughts" in accordance to whichever theory he was a fierce proponent of at the time. She understood the difference between the two well enough (thank you very much!). But Claire had still become annoyed when he tried to correct her; in her view, it did not matter too much whether you used one term over the other, even though you might mean the latter, while speaking of the former.

She shrugged away her irritation. She had become quite good at that. She had also learned that from Jannus, though not in a conscious or direct way. More an "after-the-fact" kind of deal.

Claire took a left this time, passing a secluded flower-filled area with a resting bench. She could not recall the names of the flora they cultivated here, yet she did recognise a singular rose, now faded. Almost every moment of her life (as far as she could remember), it had felt like she had had to fight to hold on. Relatively early in life she had got in with the wrong crowd, the wrong kind of people. He parents had been very absent, so Claire had been left to her own devices. There had been no immediate support or replacements for her primary caregivers, so she had searched elsewhere.

And then she had met all the wrong people. Wrong for her, anyhow. It was not until she had met Jannus that all that had changed. Thinking back on it, those beginnings had been very romantic, almost dream-like. Realism entered into it later, of course, but she would forever treasure those first days. Not that she wanted to return to them. But as a building block or guiding stone, it still served her in a positive way. *And she no longer feared the shadows, that had always haunted her. They were still there, to be sure, just beyond her sight. Yet their presence no longer filled her with terror and trepidation.*

Claire had almost reached the eastern entrance of the park area; from there she would go down to visit her best friend (*hopefully not stilling ailing from the flu*, she thought, absently touching her stomach lightly), just a few blocks down.

I wonder if she can hear the cats from there, Claire thought. *I never got around to asking her.* The sky had been sunny for a few days now, after almost a whole week with an overcast sky. Now she looked up, once again, at the cloudy sky, and felt the first few drops on her face. As she kept her face turned upward, she felt grateful.